NOT YOUR FATHER'S MAFIA

By Gunther Allen

TABLE OF CONTENTS

CHAPTER 1

Tito

In the dimly lit chambers of our family organization's home headquarters, my father Salvator Barbarotti Senior, the aging patriarch of the once-mighty crime family, grappled with the weight of decisions that loomed like shadows over his legacy. The scent of cigar smoke, thick and suffocating, clung to the air as he stared out of the window, watching the city that had both served and challenged the Barbarotti Family for decades.

My father donned the "Greasy Hands Salv" moniker and lingered on the cityscape—a tapestry he had woven through clandestine dealings. He beheld the changing tides—where legal lottery, online poker machines, and even sports gambling usurped backroom poker games. Once-forbidden substances now danced on the edge of legitimacy in the eyes of the law. My voice was a faint echo in his mind, whispering for a shift in strategy, and a new modus operandi. The ideas of iPhones, social media, and cryptocurrency, all enigmas to him, felt like deciphering a cryptic language he couldn't quite grasp. And on the North Side of Chicago, where our Barbarotti Family held sway, a power struggle awaited its spark.

As for myself, I discarded the moniker Salvator Jr. and fully embraced the illustrious mantle of Tito Barbarotti, a name that not only embodied my family's heritage but also allowed me to exude confidence and innovation. Armed with a freshly minted master's in business administration, my expertise spanned a multitude of disciplines including managerial economics, entrepreneurship, marketing, supply chain, and operations management. My formal education set me apart from the traditional mob persona my father was used to. The furrowed brow of my father betrayed the inner conflict with which he grappled—torn between embracing the evolving world and clinging to the familiar echoes of the past.

In the vibrant pulse of Chicago, as a youthful twenty-three-year-old, I effortlessly blended both strength and intellect. My lineage and Italian heritage endowed me with a chiseled, sculpted visage, accentuated by my dark, untamed locks and what some described as captivating hazel brown-green eyes. A physique reminiscent of the

Renaissance reflected my commitment to fitness, honed through spirited engagement in outdoor sports. Confidence emanated from my stride, casting a magnetic allure that captured attention. However, my father harbored reservations about what he believed was a chosen lifestyle. Despite attracting desire from women, I acknowledged my identity as a gay man navigating a world that demanded discretion. Maintaining a charismatic playboy facade, I surrounded myself with beautiful women, engaging in an intricate dance of illusion.

In my father's study, tension crackled like electricity, a conspicuous presence lingering between us, heavy with unspoken words. My father spoke to me, his disappointment evident, despite having sent me to the best boarding schools and my graduating with honors from Michigan State University—a school ranked number one in supply chain management/logistics. "Why can't you be attracted to women like everyone else?" The fact that I was attracted to men was a bitter pill for him to swallow, yet my mother, Virginia, managed to help my father be more amenable. She was no ordinary mob wife. To say she was a formidable woman would be an understatement. Her resolve matched my father Greasy Hands Salv's persona but pointed in a diffcrent direction. Within the faintly illuminated rooms where the scent of cigar smoke mingled with the tension of familial conflict, a delicate dance unfolded. Love and tension intermingled, as the matriarch subtly nudged my father toward my acceptance.

While my father remained fixated on the evolving landscape of crime, where algorithms seemed poised to replace back-alley deals, my mother remained steadfast in her focus on keeping the family together, emerging as my ardent champion. She played a pivotal role in helping my father reconcile with my slick suits and modern ideas, which symbolized a seismic shift in our world—a shift that felt as alien to him as a spaceship landing in Capone's Chicago. My father's typical retort, often peppered with negativity, reflected his struggle to adapt: "What is this world coming to," or variations like "The world's going to shit in a handcart," or "We're all going to hell in a handbasket." Despite our efforts to reassure him that change was inevitable and sometimes beneficial, my father grappled with embracing this brave new world.

I understood that implementing significant business changes would lead the family into uncharted territory, yet I harbored the belief that perhaps I had stumbled upon something that could perpetuate the

Barbarotti legacy in this digital age. As the cigar smoke, a steadfast companion in myriad moments of reflection, wafted through the air, it seemed to mirror the uncertainty shrouding the once-unassailable foundations of the Barbarotti Family.

In my father's world, the evolving trends of crime held less concern for him. His focus was on my succession to the throne of his empire, yet in his eyes, being gay equated to weakness. How could I ever be accepted as a future mob kingpin if my true identity were revealed? He feared that the revelation would shake the old-school sensibilities of mob bosses like a thunderclap echoing through a smoky speakeasy.

I had to confront my dad directly, challenging his assumptions head-on.

"Why do you always assume the worst about me and the family business? Dad, do you truly believe that my capabilities are judged solely based on who I choose to sleep with? It's absurd. You know the family respects and supports me."

My father, like often, turned away, unable to muster a rebuttal. Undeterred, I persisted day after day, hoping to sway him.

"I want the entire Barbarotti clan to accept my sexuality, but I need your full acceptance first, Dad. I've proven my strength as an athlete, excelled in debating, and effectively led teams. I'm confident the family will recognize that times have changed."

The struggles at home only fueled my determination, and despite the generational clash, I refused to apologize for embracing my true self. Slowly but surely, I aimed to change my father's perspective, one step at a time.

To an outsider, the scenario might appear amusing—a gay mobster challenging the entrenched norms of organized crime. The politically correct pronouns could easily become as entangled as a bowl of spaghetti in a mob-run kitchen. Yet, resolute in my refusal to be defined by labels, I remained steadfast in my determination and resilience, a refreshing departure from the stifling traditions upheld by the Chicago Outfit. It was a new era, and a new generation was poised to take the reins.

However, the deeply ingrained traditions of the Barbarotti Family, along with my father's reservations, posed significant obstacles. Nevertheless, it was evident that I was well-liked within the family circle, owing largely to my affable nature. Without sounding conceited, I've often been told that I possess a charm not commonly associated with a burgeoning mob boss or kingpin. Yet this charm afforded me an unconventional form of influence.

In a world where power was the ultimate currency, my vision was like a high-stakes game of Monopoly, but with better suits and fewer arguments over who gets to be the banker. I saw our organization waltzing between shadows, using technology as our trusty sidekick instead of just another pawn in the game. It was a bold departure from the old-school approach of "brawn over brains," like bringing a strategy guide to a street fight. I wasn't just some charming gay oddball in the mob, but a visionary on a mission to give the Barbarotti legacy a modern-day makeover. Think less "Mob Boss: Original Recipe" and more "Mob Boss: Special Edition."

In an underworld where tradition clung to the backstreets like stubborn chewing gum, I waltzed in with all the finesse of a tango dancer in a softly shaded speakeasy. My charm was my secret weapon, the kind that made even the toughest mobsters question their loyalty to the tried-and-true methods of the past. It was like trying to introduce gluten-free pasta in an old-school Italian restaurant—raised eyebrows, skeptical glances, but maybe, just maybe, a chance for something surprisingly delightful.

The dichotomy between the old guard and my more modern ever-shifting landscape, I stood at the crossroads of tradition and transformation of power and influence, armed with nothing but my conviction and a desire for change. With each step forward, I challenged the status quo, reshaping the very foundations of organized crime. As the echoes of the past collided with the promise of the future, I embraced the uncertainty, knowing that the legacy of the Barbarotti Family depended on my ability to adapt, innovate, and defy expectations.

Now, the one thing I was missing was my partner in crime, so to speak. Navigating the tricky waters of dating was challenging for anyone, let alone someone trying to introduce a significant other to their family—especially if that family happened to be a notorious crime organization.

"Oh, hello there. This is my father, Greasy Hands Salv. How about we all go out for Italian tonight?" Yeah, it's not your typical family dinner introduction.

CHAPTER 2

Rico

In the morning, I found myself alone in my new apartment. Tito hadn't spent the night and had likely returned home after watching me fall fast asleep. My mind raced in every direction until I saw that Tito had left a note.

I'm sorry I had to leave, but I have family commitments in the morning. Sunday tradition called for brunch with the "familia." But if you're not busy, perhaps we can get together for dinner tonight? I'll give you a call later.

I reflected on yesterday and how innocently I'd found Tito. It wasn't as if I was trolling Grindr for leads or anything of the sort. Having moved to a new city, I felt lonely and was navigating the awkward waters of meeting people in the digital age. My intentions were far from just hooking up. I was exploring opportunities and seeing if anything promising caught my eye.

My inbox was flooded with messages, most of which were either straightforward requests for quick hookups or mundane "What are you up to?" inquiries. Nevertheless, Tito's message stood out from all the rest. It was a simple inquiry asking if I was new in town. Was Tito clairvoyant, or did he keep track of everyone in the area? My psychology training kicked in, and I found myself over-analyzing everything—an admitted fault of mine in life.

Now, I suddenly found myself with a big smile on my face, put on my jogging shorts and running shoes, and made my exit from the elevators of my building, ready to hit the trail to the River Walk and embark on a new routine of running—a daily ritual for the past decade or so. Moving had disrupted my workout regimen, and I hadn't even checked out the fully equipped gym in the building. I hoped that after finishing my jog, I could squeeze in an easy weight workout as well. I still sported a big smile as I put in my earbuds, reflecting on every detail of the events of the past twenty-four hours.

I believed I had a lot to offer. I was a rookie who had graduated at the top of my class in the Criminal Investigation Division, specializing in organized crime and those involved in human and drug trafficking. I had also earned a criminal psychology BA from the University of California at Irvine. Despite my young age of twenty-four, I had already weathered three years in the trenches of criminal law before the FBI beckoned.

It was Sunday, and I had yet to unpack all my things, getting ready for my first full week at my new job. Unfortunately—or fortunately, depending on how you look at it—I found myself too occupied getting unorganized, messing up the place instead of organizing and unpacking thanks to my encounter with Tito. Well, unless you considered unpacking other things; that were wound up rather tightly.

Regardless, the evening had turned out to be a very pleasant surprise, and I happily anticipated a rendezvous with Tito later for dinner. I cranked up the music, picked up the pace, and quickly lengthened my stride, heading down the River Walk towards the mouth of Lake Michigan. The city around me faded into the rhythm of my steps, and the day held the promise of both routine and romantic unpredictability.

I found myself interrupted by a phone call from my new boss at the FBI. The FBI had urgent information for me that needed preparation before Monday's crucial meeting. The head of my department's task force on organized crime, Lieutenant Herman Guild, had acquired insider intel suggesting that the Barbarotti Crime Family was undergoing significant changes in their operations. Rumors swirled that the kingpin, Greasy Hands Salv, was contemplating stepping down and passing the reins to his son. Despite being a mere twenty-three years old, the young successor was deemed a smart cookie, poised to innovate the criminal operation into the 21st century.

Lieutenant Guild intended to place me along with my new partner and roommate Liz as the lead investigators to infiltrate the inner sanctum of the Barbarotti Crime Family. Our mission was to uncover the details of the operation and assess the involvement of this new, enigmatic young man in suspected criminal activities that might include murder, racketeering, prostitution, gambling, and human smuggling.

I decided to prioritize other matters for now. I headed to the gym, determined to put my apartment in order and get ready for my hot date by getting pumped and creating an HGTV-Decor-styled apartment.

As I finished my workout, I noticed the new phone number I'd put into his phone yesterday lighting up. Eagerly answering, I couldn't help but smile at Tito's saying "hello."

"Hey handsome," I responded, "How was your brunch? Did everything go well?"

Tito's enthusiasm was noticeable. "Everything went better than I ever expected. I was hoping that my dad would be receptive to some new ideas, but I didn't expect things to move so well."

I could sense Tito's excitement and felt a surge of happiness for him. "This calls for a celebration! I heard of a place near the Theater District that my boss recommended, and I'd love to take you there tonight. It's called Wildfire Restaurant; do you know it?"

Tito, sounded equally thrilled, "Know it? It's one of my favorite spots in the city and a perfect choice."

"Is it casual, or do we need a dinner coat, or something even more formal?"

"Not to worry. Casual is fine, and a dinner coat works, too. Wear what feels comfortable, and I can't wait until tonight!"

* * * *

Tito

Earlier in the day, I was undergoing a process of revelations and excitement in preparation for my family gathering—a transition to a new way of thinking and an unveiling of the world's first major global carbon-neutral blockchain connecting businesses, including the emerging cannabidiol (CBD) and marijuana industry, all within the framework of regulatory institutions. Essentially, the world was embracing industries once persecuted and dismissed as evil, now hailed as bastions of health—offering benefits from better sleep to relief for those with migraines. Yes, it was a new world, and one I was excited to share with my dad and the rest of the family.

Oh, I also had things to share with my mom regarding Rico, but for now, I was busy putting together a spreadsheet to show my dad. I harbored the idea of starting my very own cryptocurrency under the guise of a corporate finance institute.

To begin with, I recognized the complexities and time constraints involved in launching one's own blockchain. Alternatively, I also considered utilizing established platforms like the Ethereum network, Solana, or Ripple, which allowed for the creation of new cryptocurrencies on their existing blockchains. While this approach provided less flexibility in customizing a token, it emerged as a more straightforward method for initiating a new blockchain.

Nonetheless, I acknowledged the drawback: the cryptocurrency's reliance on the chosen blockchain. If the selected blockchain experienced any issues or failures, the ability to conduct transactions with the token would be compromised. Eager to explore these ideas further, I planned to discuss them with my father and other family members within the organization.

With the increased pressure on regulators to clamp down on cryptocurrencies, ensuring that whatever we chose to use would be accepted as an allowed cryptocurrency was crucial. For instance, China did not allow any, but hey I figured we didn't do business with China anyhow. These were thoughts I'd soon discuss over brunch, hoping the scrambled eggs would be as easily digestible as my business ideas.

Every family gathering unfurls into a culinary extravaganza, a gastronomic spectacle in which everyone participates alongside their spouses. Each brings dishes to the table, sparking spirited arguments over whose creation reigns supreme—a friendly banter ritual performed religiously, even though none of us are devout followers.

In earlier times, the entire family would attend Mass before the feast, but the Church's entanglement in scandals, including pedophilia and other unsavory controversies, led the Catholic Church to believe that hosting the mob wasn't in their best interest. Yet, a historical connection between the mob and the Church lingered, echoing the deep-seated corruption within Chicago's network. Times had changed, however, with many now gravitating toward businesses better suited to regulations and scrutiny.

As a visionary, I decided to focus on the burgeoning CBD oil industry and the expanding legalized marijuana market. Integrating these ventures into my blockchain security concepts became paramount. Sensing the urgency to launch these initiatives before potential competitors, including the Russians, gained traction, I was propelled into action. The landscape of Chicago's underworld was shifting, and I was resolute in my determination not to lag behind in this high-stakes game, where each strategic move could either fortify or imperil the family legacy.

Once everyone was comfortably seated and full of another epic Sunday brunch, it was time to shift into some family business. Concealed to just me, my father began to let everyone know that he was gearing up to step down and hand over the reins to the new generation of thinkers.

First, he appointed me to lead the charge on new operations, stating, "Until everything starts running smoothly, it's business as usual. Then, gradually, we'll phase out the old business when the new revenues prove to be a feasible and as lucrative alternative as we hope."

At this point, rising to my feet, I delivered an impassioned speech about my blockchain ideas. I unveiled plans for a CBD and marijuana division, aiming to also supply the unregulated herbal supplement kratom—often promoted as a natural alternative pain remedy, despite containing the same chemicals found in opioids, yet legal.

Envisioning a future pharmaceutical division, contingent on acquiring the necessary lab equipment, I acknowledged this wouldn't happen overnight but confidently detailed plans for phasing in CBD products. Behind the scenes, coordination with marketing and supply partners from previous business relationships had already begun. As I laid out the blueprint for a smooth transition, one of my many uncles couldn't contain himself and yelled out, "Smooth Tito!" My new recently adopted moniker resonated as epic as a new brand of vodka.

I was so thrilled that I couldn't wait to share my news with Rico. While I hadn't explicitly mentioned the details, I hinted that I would be sharing some exciting updates at my bi-monthly traditional family brunch meeting, even though we always gathered with immediate family every Sunday. Anyhow, I just couldn't wait to share the news and decided to give Rico a call.

* * * *

As the clock struck dinner time, I had already called Rico and was preparing to whisk him away to Wildfire Restaurant, where I had already made reservations. Pulling up in my sleek, all-black Tesla, its silent purr and luxurious interior exuded sophistication and power. I could practically feel Rico's stunned expression as he took in the sight of my impressive ride. Anticipation bubbled within me as I imagined the evening ahead, filled with good food, laughter, and the promise of something special between us.

As Rico hopped in, he mentioned, "I've never ridden in a Tesla before, but I've always wanted to. This is incredible with the large screen, and your steering wheel looks like the controls of a spaceship!"

I gave Rico the ten-cent tour and explained all the unique features, "This wheel, actually called the steering yoke, is an extra addition, and you can get a regular model with the traditional steering wheel to drive. All my controls are touchscreen—forward, backward, side mirrors, etc."

Rico seemed genuinely impressed, thoroughly enjoying the futuristic experience. As I accelerated, effortlessly propelling the all-electric car to sixty MPH, Rico's head snapped back into the seat. "Wow, this has power," he remarked, his tone filled with genuine awe. Then, with a playful grin, he added, "Sort of reminds me of something else that surges forward in a second."

I couldn't help but chuckle, teasingly responding, "Well, I guess the thrust in your engine does rise quickly!"

Rico shot back with a smirk, "Guilty as charged, but it's all your fault."

I raised an eyebrow, feigning innocence, "What do you mean 'my fault?'"

"When you go around looking as hot as you do, you're responsible for others' actions."

I couldn't contain my grin. "What are you talking about?"

"It's called accountability—the state of being responsible for something that you've caused!"

Our laughter filled the car, setting the tone for another delightful evening together.

The dinner was as enchanting as the company, and the vintage 1920s décor lent a romantic atmosphere, further heightened by a couple of Raspberry Cosmos that slid down with ease. As the evening unfolded, I could sense by Rico's hungry expression that he couldn't help but wonder where it would lead—and I wasn't talking about hunger for food. Would we head back to his apartment, or would I unveil my place? Simultaneously, I posed the question to Rico: "Should we go to your place or mine? I promise my place doesn't offer as spectacular a view as yours, but I'm sure I could show you something else interesting to look at."

"Ha ha, nothing that I haven't already seen, but it's definitely worth a second look."

I then chauffeured us to my brownstone, a stone's throw away from Wrigley Field, the Cub's baseball team's home stadium. My residence was a nostalgic ode to old Chicago, with charming streets, intricate stone carvings, cornices, and elaborate ironwork—ageless architectural gems that seamlessly blended timeless elegance with modern chic. I watched Rico, who likely felt transported to a bygone era of romance, surrounded by the French Romanesque style of architecture.

As we entered, Rico couldn't help but ask, "So, which way to your bedroom?"

I whimsically orchestrated a playful game of strip, leaving behind a breadcrumb trail of clothing—shoes, coat, shirt, pants, undershirt, underpants, and, finally, socks. Each discarded garment marked our progression towards the bedroom, where Rico, catching onto the tantalizing tease, eagerly followed suit. This set the stage for what I hoped would be an evening of shared intimacy in the blossoming embrace of our romance.

As we stood there, the air between us thick with anticipation, I couldn't help but be drawn to Rico's magnetic presence. His eyes held a fiery intensity, reflecting the desire that burned within me. But that wasn't the only thing that was intense as he stood there fully nude and erect with desire.

His uncut personality intrigued me, as it was my first time experiencing someone uncut, and I'm not just talking about an unfiltered personality. It was the raw excitement of something different, and I found myself completely thrilled and even fascinated, which only served to turn me on even more. Within seconds we explored each other's bodies with lingering touches, and the tension between us mounted, electrifying the atmosphere with raw passion.

I traced the contours of Rico's body with gentle fingertips, committing every curve and shape as if committing them to memory. His muscles were firm yet warm to my touch; they seemed to ignite beneath my fingertips, hard and sturdy, and they fueled the flames of desire that raged within me.

Rico held out a condom he had somehow plucked out of a pocket while shedding his clothes, but I let him know it wouldn't be necessary. His eyes filled with deep concern, and I immediately reassured him. "I've been on PrEP for a while now, and the last time I was checked, I tested negative several months ago. Since then, there hasn't been any action except for you."

Rico, visibly relieved, interjected, "I'm negative as well. The last time I checked was over a year ago, but I've been swamped with school and work. I know…please don't say it…I'm a bit out of practice."

I understood exactly where Rico was coming from and stopped the conversation to avoid spoiling the moment. With each kiss, each caress, I surrendered a little more to the intoxicating pull of lust, losing myself in the passion of the moment.

The room seemed to fade away, leaving only the two of us suspended in a world of pleasure. Every touch, every whisper, was a testament to the depth of our connection, kindling an inferno that threatened to consume me.

Rico grabbed me from behind and squeezed me slowly and firmly while entering. He started inching his way inside me, and his hard throbs sent sensations throughout my body. I wanted all of him, but I had never had someone as large try before.

Suddenly, time stood still, allowing me to savor every inch of Rico's hunger. Moans of shared intimacy arose, and sounds of satisfaction and bliss filled the sultry zephyr.

Our innermost yearnings caused us to quicken as our pace and vigor became more rapid. The pounding rhythm relentlessly continued to build, and we both lost control in the moment, as if animal instinct had taken hold of us.

In the culmination of our longing, our bodies fused and succumbed to the rapturous ecstasy of our union. Every touch and caress ignited an inferno of sensation that melded our spirits. It was as if we both descended into the depths of our shared yearning, our souls intertwining into a singular, pulsating entity at the zenith of our carnal fervor.

With a shared sigh of contentment, we relished our exhilarating climax, our bodies still humming with the electricity; as the world gradually reappeared around us, we savored the euphoria of our triumph.

We both lay there, basking in the afterglow, mesmerized by the depth of our connection. It felt like we had reached a pinnacle of both pleasure and contentment that neither of us had ever experienced. As I gazed into Rico's eyes, I felt an overwhelming urge to express just how incredible the moment was.

"This…this was fucking incredible!" I exclaimed, my voice tinged with awe and wonder. "I don't think I've ever felt this way before. I could lie here with you forever."

Rico's eyes sparkled with agreement. "You're not kidding," he said, his voice husky with emotion. "That was a twenty on a scale of one to ten! I wish it could go on forever as well."

But reality intruded, a harsh reminder of responsibilities and obligations. I glanced at the clock and realized with a sinking feeling that morning was fast approaching. Rico had to get up early for work, and as much as I wanted to cling to this moment, I knew he couldn't stay. As he reluctantly began to stir, a pang of reluctance swept over me. I wanted to hold onto him, to freeze time in this perfect bubble of intimacy.

But duty called, and with a heavy heart, I watched as Rico prepared to leave, the promise of another day looming on the horizon. Though Rico would have loved to spend the entire night and wake up in my arms, he regretted that he had early morning commitments which seemed to weigh on him. He reluctantly asked if I could give him a lift back to his apartment before it got too late.

"Please, don't go," I pleaded, knowing all too well that Monday morning would soon shatter our idyllic bubble and force us back into the harsh reality of the daily grind.

Rico expressed his gratitude to me for the wonderful evening, and I reciprocated, thanking Rico for a fantastic celebration.

After we got dressed and I drove him to his apartment as requested I repeated my thanks. "Just being with you was celebration enough." I was hoping that he would fall for my smooth, kitschy romantic ways.

And by how passionate his goodbye kiss was, I believe it was working.

* * * *

Rico

Back home, my mind was consumed by memories of our passionate lovemaking. Despite the ache of parting, I rode the elevator to the ninetieth floor, preparing for the day ahead. My closet offered an array of neatly pressed white shirts, and I selected a tie to match my mood, opting for red and blue in a nod to tradition, as I was reminiscent of the magical evening I had just experienced.

As I settled into bed, the lingering scent of Tito's cologne enveloped me, weaving through my thoughts and memories. Despite a twinge of loneliness, I found solace in the lingering echoes of our time together. As I succumbed to the tender embrace of slumber, I embarked on a voyage through the whimsical realms of my dreams, my heart pulsating with eager anticipation for my next rendezvous with Tito.

CHAPTER 3

Rico

Hitting the alarm set me into automatic get-ready mode. I still felt a little disoriented in my new surroundings, but I welcomed my huge walk-in shower with its overhead rain head and massage jets that were a huge step up from the tub shower I had back home in California. All these perks for getting such a prestigious position on the FBI's organized crime task force. FBI agent's median salaries for the past few years run around $69K a year plus commissions, bonuses, and profit-sharing.

Working on a special task force afforded me a bit more base pay, along with the added perk of free housing, which I found immensely advantageous. The prospect of covering the cost of such accommodations solely on my salary seemed farfetched. Furthermore, I found myself sharing the living space with a roommate I had yet to encounter. Pondering Liz's whereabouts, I mused, "Where in the world could she be, anyway?"

Confident that she would surface for the meeting, I remained unruffled. I trusted that everything would fall into place, or at least I hoped so. At twenty-four years old, I recognized the privilege of my circumstances and approached my responsibilities with diligence. Prepared to not only arrive on time but to come in early, I awaited the details of my assignment, eager to learn what it would entail to infiltrate the Barbarotti crime family.

I found myself in the FBI headquarters earlier than I imagined; it was only a brief drive from my city apartment. Fortunately, the route I took spared me from the dreaded freeways that often turned into nightmarish traffic jams, or so I had heard. My destination was the Near West Side, just on the other side of the University of Illinois off Roosevelt Rd., past the 90 Freeway that circled downtown Chicago.

Arriving a generous thirty minutes ahead of schedule, I took a moment to relax and enjoy a cup of coffee, tending to the required forms and security clearances that needed to be signed. My boss, Lieutenant Guild, entered the room and greeted me as I navigated the bureaucratic process.

"Good morning, Mr. Baas. I trust you had a good weekend. Are you all settled into your new place? Is everything to your liking?"

"Yes, sir, I had a pleasant weekend," I replied, "and I'm all settled in now, but I still haven't met Liz, my partner. The new digs are wonderful—very impressive."

Lt. Guild nodded, "I bet they are, son. No other employees get the perks you and Liz are receiving for this task force. But remember, it's part of your undercover assignment, so don't get too comfortable. It is an honor, son, don't forget that."

"I won't, sir," I assured him.

"Now we have important matters to discuss, and we all need to meet in the briefing room," Lt. Guild announced as he handed me a packet of papers, including a dossier. Here is your information sheet with names, Venn diagrams, and the family tree of the Barbarotti Family."

As I perused the dossier, I took a sip of coffee. Suddenly, I choked and sprayed coffee all over the floor, my heart plummeting into my stomach as the realization hit me like a freight train. The man I had been entangled with romantically was none other than the very target of the investigation. Shock, disbelief, and a profound sense of betrayal washed over me, leaving me reeling in a cyclone of emotions.

Lt. Guild's concerned gaze bore into me. "You okay, son?"

I forced a smile. "Yes, sir, just went down the wrong way."

But inside, turmoil raged. The face I had just been intimate with was now staring back at me from the dossier as the next in line to lead the Barbarotti Family—"Smooth Tito Barbarotti."

How could this be? It was beyond coincidental. I now wondered if this was all a setup and if Tito played me like a deck of cards. I knew I couldn't say anything and risk losing my position on the first day. Determined, I was resolved not only to investigate but to find out, "Does Tito have true feelings for me or not?"

During the briefing, I heard words suggesting that Tito might be a killer and a thief, even though there was no hard evidence. Wanting clarification, I asked Lt. Guild, "What is the evidence of any infractions by Mr. Salvador Jr., aka Tito Barbarotti? Does he have a rap sheet? Any warrants? Arrests? Has he broken any laws, or does he have a criminal record?"

The Lieutenant became agitated, "We have nothing on Tito yet, but I feel it is only a matter of time. Everyone in that family eventually ends up spending at least some time behind bars."

Unconvinced, I remarked, "So, you are basing all your accusations on supposition and innuendos. If I am to investigate Tito and find out the absolute truth, then I should be given the absolute truth as well."

The entire task force, about fifteen people, turned their eyes on me. It was the first time they had seen anyone question Lt. Guild.

"Touché, Agent Baas, well spoken," Lt. Guild replied. "That's why I expect a thorough report each and every day about what you learn about this man, his family members, and what they are up to…understood?"

I confidently replied, "Yes, sir!"

Just then, a statuesque woman with a commanding presence strolled into the meeting, catching everyone's attention. Lt. Guild, with his typical gravitas, announced, "Just in time, Special Agent Doucet. I want you to meet your new partner, Rico Bass."

I rose from my seat, extending a hand in greeting, while Lt. Guild seamlessly continued, "Agent Bass, this is Agent Liz Doucet— your new partner and roommate. Agent Doucet has graced us with her expertise on a couple of other task forces, including orchestrating a successful FBI sting operation at the Chicago Mercantile Exchange, exposing fraud, and unveiling rigged trades. I anticipate you two working in harmony and endeavoring to befriend the young Salvador Jr., known as the city's most dashing playboy."

Now, the ball rested firmly in my court, and I grappled with the daunting task ahead. I had to reveal to Liz, my new partner, that I was gay, and that Tito, their target, shared the same orientation. How could I navigate the intricate dance of explaining that I had already woven myself into Tito's life?

The challenge loomed larger as I pondered how to continue my relationship with Tito, all while keeping the nature of my profession veiled. As I mulled over my options, I concluded that honesty was my best course of action. With this resolve in mind, I turned to Liz, asking, "Could we meet after the briefing?"

As soon as the briefing had concluded, Lt. Guild saw an opportunity for me and Liz to delve into our assignment. With a hint of humor, he remarked, "No pun intended, but you two need to get intimately familiar with the details in those packets and dossiers you've got there. Any questions, bring them straight to me—pun entirely intended. Now, I know you're both gay, and that's not why I paired you up. Still, it might just work in our favor."

I was taken aback but now it seemed even more appropriate to lay it all on the table right in front of my new roommate and my boss. I confessed, "Lt. Guild, I've serendipitously started a relationship with Tito. Yep, turns out he swings my way, too. In fact, we hit it off on Grindr, of all places. All that Playboy charm? Just a front. And you know what? I believe we actually like each other!"

The Lieutenant's eyes widened, and he exclaimed, "Well, this is a first, something like this has never happened before. You're telling me you had no idea you were assigned to get close to Smooth Tito Barbarotti."

I replied, "No, Lt. Guild, I had absolutely no clue. I was alone in the apartment, lonely, and just wanted to meet someone. Oh, shit, this is not coming out right!"

Liz chimed in, her tone conveying surprise, "Honestly, I live with my girlfriend, and the roommate situation is just for cover. You probably won't be seeing me at the condo, except for work reasons related to this case. Going solo might be to the FBI's advantage."

The Lieutenant's expression remained one of shock as he requested, "I need further details…Rico, you need to dig deeper into the Barbarotti family and find out from Tito what they do for a living."

Deep down, I sensed that Tito was a genuinely good person. The real dilemma lay in determining whether I could trust my instincts or if my judgment was clouded by mere physical attraction. However, I knew I had a job to do, so I laid out my case, "I think I should just let the relationship play out naturally because I believe that Tito genuinely likes me and has already mentioned to me about meeting his family."

Both Liz and the Lieutenant were impressed and almost in unison said, "Boy, you sure are a fast worker, aren't you!" Plus, they both had stupid grins on their faces.

I continued, "Ha ha… I think in this case, the heart knows what it wants, and from what I have seen so far, I think you'll both be surprised to know that Tito wants the family to become a legitimate business operation and steer away from the "Crime Family Model.""

The Lieutenant responded to me, saying, "Well, we all hope for a positive outcome son, but let's not act naïve and jump the gun on what could or might unfold. You seem to have already developed a relationship that is progressing quickly, indicating that Tito trusts you. Maintain that trust.

Do you have any reservations about going solo and continuing your investigation? By the way, I was serious about documenting everything you learn. We need thorough corroboration."

Rico responded, "Sir, I'm fully committed to the mission, and I'll ensure thorough documentation. In case I find myself spending nights together, with Tito, I can provide voice-recorded updates on my phone to capture the intricacies of unfolding developments."

Lt. Guild nodded in agreement and concern and said, "Keep us apprised of any noteworthy events… I don't need to know your play-by-play, but any changes, or insights into ongoing operations are crucial. Understand?"

I replied, "Understood!"

Liz assured me that she was there to support me in any way possible. While she wouldn't visit the apartment unless necessary, it could serve as a discreet means for me to pass on information if reporting to headquarters became challenging. Anticipating that the Barbarotti Family might scrutinize me once they learned of my relationship with Tito, Liz cautioned, "You're essentially living with the enemy. Stay stealthy and be hyper-aware of every move, as it might be checked out by the Barbarotti Family."

I concurred, "I'll act normal and be myself, with one minor detail hidden—my employment with the FBI. If they dig into my past, they'll find I've worked as a psychologist in criminal law. I could say

I'm currently working as a criminal law psychologist for a law firm or something."

Liz nodded approvingly, "That's a perfect idea. Keep it as close to the truth as possible, and I'll explore connecting you with an undercover position in a law firm here in Chicago."

* * * *

Tito

I found myself deeply immersed in the delicate task of persuading my family to embrace a path of legitimacy. I believed that transitioning to a lawful organization could yield both legal and financial benefits, a proposition I was determined to sell to my father and the rest of the family.

As the video slot machine sector was booming, I pivoted towards the burgeoning CBD oil industry, seeing it as a potential avenue for the Barbarotti Family's ventures. Despite the legalization of once-illicit activities like sports betting, which had become highly profitable, our family business recognized the need to adapt to this changing landscape. My family could no longer compete since online betting was available to everyone. With the promise of substantial financial gains, I aimed to capitalize on this shift by exploring legitimate business opportunities, seeking to rejuvenate our traditional mafia business model.

I recognized the dominance of corporate greed in the world and sought nothing more than securing a small piece of the action for myself and my family—a pursuit aligned with the evolving American dream. All it would take is combining some of the latest AI and blockchain tweaks to make everything available at the touch of a smartphone.

I wanted to share my idea with Rico as well, but I had to be careful and delicately dance around the true nature of my family's business and the events unfolding. Sharing how I engage in discussions with my father's associates and laying the groundwork for my innovative ideas would work in any type of business, so if I generalized, I figured it would be okay.

Besides, my goal was to transition from traditional mafia activities to legitimate business ventures, considering what was deemed illegal was gradually becoming socially acceptable anyway. What harm would there be if I just called Rico and let him know how my day was going?

* * * *

Rico

I noticed my phone ringing and lit up once he saw who the caller was. Tito and I talked all about his meeting with his family and how things went. I had learned how to be a good listener and not share too much about myself and of course nothing about being part of an FBI task force.

As we hung up, I couldn't shake the weight of the conversation from my mind. I sensed how sincere Tito was about sharing his life, but I felt conflicted between my job and a lingering unease about certain secrets I harbored about my work with the FBI that I couldn't divulge.

The gravity of these unspoken truths pressed heavily on my conscience, casting shadows of doubt over my burgeoning relationship with Tito. I now found myself standing at a crucial juncture, my heart heavy with the truth I wanted to unveil—to the man who was slowly and surely weaving his way into my thoughts and feelings.

I called back into the FBI headquarters, grappling with the knowledge that a full report for Lieutenant Guild awaited him. The dilemma loomed–what should I disclose? My conscience tugged me in conflicting directions, yet the undeniable truth persisted: Tito hadn't committed any wrongdoing. In the realm of transparency, Tito emerged as the unsung hero of this unfolding narrative.

My task was clear—to illustrate conclusively that the Barbarotti Family was steering toward the path of rectitude. They were transforming into a legitimate business, dutifully paying taxes, adhering to regulations, and abandoning any inclination to dispose of inconvenient bodies.

The corporate world itself proved ruthless enough, with winners showing no mercy, but such ruthlessness didn't fall under the FBI's purview unless tainted by fraud. Up to this point, I could only convey that no fraudulent activities were on the horizon for Smooth Tito. It appeared, even at the inception of this investigation, that this might be an operation that did not need any further probing.

Upon perusing my report, Lieutenant Guild found himself in a state of perplexity. The eloquently written document offered a comprehensive account of the Barbarotti Family's operations in just a couple days, leaving the lieutenant bewildered.

He turned to me, questioning, "How on earth did you manage to get this close, this quickly, and gather such intricate details?"

I responded nonchalantly, "Well Tito seems to want to share everything with me and wants to be transparent and honest, and I also ascertained his strong attraction toward me. I'll let you draw your own conclusions, but it's an age-old tactic in covert operations to swiftly gain essential details—become intimately acquainted with your adversary. But in this case, I also have strong feelings for Tito."

"In short," I insisted, "Mr. Tito Barbarotti is a good young man with no record who is turning his family into an honest running business if you exclude the dirty business practices that ninety-nine percent of corporations use today to get on top. It is the new American way of life. Dog eat dog and do anything within the law to claw your way up. There is nothing here for the FBI to question—no fraud, no money laundering. The money comes in by selling legal products, and the Barbarotti operation is merely at the cutting edge of several newly legalized businesses like growing marijuana for medical reasons and the same with CBD oils.

I have to give Tito credos for using blockchain technology that is so cutting-edge that the U.S. Government is still trying to put together regulations. Tito is well aware of this and is trying to be crystal clear about maintaining and taking over this corner of the market. Sounds like the American Dream to me!"

The Lieutenant had to hand it to me and remarked, "Well, well, Mr. Baas! Frankly, I didn't expect this side of you! In the world of the Mafia, your moniker should be "Rico Bad Ass" or "Good Ass," depending on how things play out, huh? It seems you're developing a liking for this guy. Not the most ethical move for someone under investigation, but who knows, maybe this can work in our favor. If anything pops up in the future, you can jump on it right away. Catch my drift?"

I rolled my eyes in disbelief. Was my boss cracking cheeky sexual jokes? Oh, the quirks of Chicago's way of handling things! Nevertheless, it appeared I was still part of the task force. The only twist was that our focus was now shifting to a more general direction and not just on one family operation.

I felt like the monkey had finally leaped off my back. Now, all I had to do was reveal to Tito the nature of my profession. The looming question: How would Tito react upon learning about my affiliation with criminal law? Undoubtedly, I had spared the Barbarotti Family from an extensive investigation, or as Tito humorously referred to it, "uncovering every skeleton in the closet."

However, I wasn't ready to risk the relationship until I was certain that Tito would accept me in whatever capacity I held. Opting for a more subtle approach, I decided to share the cover story Liz and I concocted a few days ago. I would tell Tito that I worked as a criminal law psychologist for a law firm, a strategic move to maintain proximity while keeping certain aspects under wraps.

I needed to come up with the law firm's name, so I gave Liz a call to get the details.

Liz picked up her phone, her voice lightening as soon as she heard my request. "I've got just the thing for you," she said. "There's a firm in Chicago—Wilson & Lambert PC. They specialize in Corporate, Government, Labor, and Employment litigation. I think this cover should work well. Plus, we've set up a convincing paper trail, just in case anyone starts digging into your background."

Both Liz and I understood that this subtle cover story was necessary to maintain my proximity to Tito, while still keeping the truth within plausible bounds. This way, we could stay under the radar and avoid raising any suspicion.

It was time to confront the situation, and I eagerly anticipated reuniting with my good friend, hoping it might lead to something more—perhaps even a romantic relationship. I thought to myself that it might seem like an unusual pairing—a criminal law psychologist dating the son of a Mafia Kingpin—but history has shown stranger alliances, especially considering the Mafia's past ties with the Church and Government Officials. Besides, I reasoned, the rule about not dating the enemy only applies when laws are broken: "As far as I can see, that's not the case here."

As I further contemplated the situation, I thought, "I'm more apprehensive about winning over Tito's family than Tito himself. The family was already undergoing significant changes. How would they handle the revelation that their son is dating me if they found out I'm really an FBI agent?"

CHAPTER 4

Tito

Rico was the first person I called to share my information about the family meeting with, but I dared not share the whole truth about what the Barbarotti Family business was. However, as I explained to Rico, all the things I was trying to accomplish with the Family Business and what I envision the business becoming.

Rico started taking deep breaths, a sure sign that something was on his mind. When he told me he had something very important to discuss, my thoughts raced—what could he have discovered?

Rico began by revealing that he had come across some unsettling information about the Barbarotti Family. He asked me, "Is it true?"

After a brief pause, I replied, "Oh, Rico, I knew it was just a matter of time before you'd find out, but I couldn't exactly start by saying my family has been in the Mafia business for the past seventy-five years. Please forgive me. I planned to tell you once we got to know each other better."

Rico explained that he did a simple background search and found out stuff about the Barbarotti Crime Family on his computer. Details about my dad, Greasy Hands Salv, and how he had been arrested multiple times for conducting mafia activities, including extortion, bribery, and illegal drug sales of marijuana.

I tried to lessen the blow by saying, "My dad is retiring from the business soon, pot is now legal, and I'm turning the operation around into a legitimized business model. Honestly, I wanted to tell you, but I didn't want to scare you away without you getting to know me a little better. I want you to trust me, but I was scared it would send you running in the other direction."

Rico responded, "Tito, I believe you, but I think we need to sit down together and be honest with each other—both of us. I haven't told you everything about me either, and I need to be clear with you as well. What do you say we lay all our cards on the table and find out if we believe we should continue getting to know each other?"

Upon hearing this, I felt a wave of mixed emotions. Fortunately, Rico learning about my ties to the Barbarotti crime family didn't prompt him to flee, especially as our relationship was just blossoming. We ended the call and all I wanted was to hold Rico in my arms and express the deep feelings I already harbored. I felt so relieved that he wasn't put off right at the get-go.

Meanwhile, my work endeavors were advancing at an accelerated pace, much faster than I had anticipated. I had skillfully secured suppliers for the CBD products I intended to distribute, utilizing my father's established distribution channels. Simultaneously, the groundwork for the online connections to my blockchain payment structure was well underway. For the time being, it allowed for Bitcoin and Ethereum as acceptable forms of payment. My ultimate aim was to establish our own cryptocurrency exchange, ensuring robust security, regulatory compliance, and advanced trading features with a global reach.

But right now, my primary desire is to reconcile things with Rico. Since I was missing him, I decided to call him back and see if we could arrange a meeting.

Rico saw my name on his phone and promptly answered, "I was just about to call you; it seems we're on the same wavelength."

I wanted to ensure that Rico was still on board with the idea of coming clean about my family's past business practices. I proposed a meeting at his place and playfully hinted at the possibility of some make-up activities.

Excited about the prospect, Rico suggested six P.M. for our get-together and teased, "Maybe you'll get a home-cooked meal if you're lucky."

Of course, I agreed, offering to bring wine and dessert while inquiring about the menu for a suitable wine pairing.

The date was set, prompting Rico to rush home to prepare the menu. About an hour later I received a text from him giving me the evening's cuisine. Knowing my fondness for the halibut at Wildfire, Rico was planning to make Halibut Almondine with Lemon Garlic Butter. He also mentioned there would be string beans, a side salad, and risotto pasta.

Rico was hosting for the first time at his new place, and it was incredibly sweet and thoughtful of him. I knew he was still adjusting to the new kitchen equipped with state-of-the-art appliances like the Gaggenau Wall Speed Oven, and Five-burner Gas Cooktop.

My fingers were crossed that he'd quickly learn how to navigate the intricacies of the speed oven for perfection in his cooking. I was also curious about what other revelations he had in store, hoping the evening would unfold smoothly and that our meal and my dessert surprise would be a huge success.

At six P.M., I arrived at the St. Regis and made my way up to the ninetieth floor. Upon reaching Rico's door, I presented a bouquet of gladiola flowers and a bottle of Pinot Noir, the perfect accompaniment to the evening's planned meal. As I stood there, I could feel the anticipation of the night buzzing around us. Ever the charmer, I inquired about our dinner plans and couldn't resist asking the burning question—would roommate Liz be joining us for the evening soirée?

Rico, aiming for transparency, responded with a casual smile, "Oh, Liz? She's got a hot date with her lucky lady, leaving the apartment all to us. We've got the bachelor pad vibe going tonight!"

I loved Rico's snug two-bedroom space. Though not sprawling, it boasted a million-dollar view of the city, including a near-wrap-around panorama of Lake Michigan and the Navy Pier. Suddenly, Rico transitioned from a playful revelation to a more serious tone.

Rico began solemnly, "I have some news about who I work for."

Having foreknowledge, I pre-empted Rico's revelation, saying, "You mean that you work at a criminal law office?"

Rico turned pale, "You already know? How long have you known for, and when were you going to say something?"

Smirking, I responded, "I, too, have my sources, and I've known for a while already. That's one of the things about my family— annoying yet revealing."

I pressed on, "I figured once you got a glimpse of my grand plans, you'd be on board. Besides, I really like you!"

Rico caught off guard but not entirely shocked, quipped, "I had a feeling that you knew more, but I'm more shocked you waited this long. Just so you know, my little investigative adventure into your family turned up nothing but gold stars for you! Now the genie is out of the bottle, we can be open about everything." Rico, locking eyes with Tito, teased, "So, you're into me, huh? Well, guess what? The feeling's mutual!"

Rico mulled over my understanding of his role as a criminal law psychologist, but I subtly shifted the topic, suggesting, "How about we both agree to steer clear of work-related talk?"

Rico immediately shifted his focus, "So, any ideas on how we navigate this mutual attraction?"

With a playful grin, I suggested, "How about we continue dating and see where this ride takes us? By the way, I've never had a boyfriend before."

"Fantastic," Rico responded, "You're my first, too, and maybe down the line, we can brave the family introductions unless you get tired of me first."

I chuckled, "Well, I don't see that happening—getting tired of you I mean. In fact, I'd love for you to meet my sprawling and eccentric family, but brace yourself; they're a lively and crazy bunch, and there's a lot of them."

Rico and I exchanged smiles and toasted to new beginnings and being honest. As the evening progressed and the burden of secrecy eased, Rico and I felt a sense of liberation and excitement.

After our sumptuous dinner, Rico's curiosity was piqued by the tantalizing promise of dessert. "I thought you mentioned dessert, Tito," he quipped.

Flashing a mischievous grin, I returned, "Oh, dessert comes with a ribbon tied around it, but it's reserved for the bedroom."

Rico, thinking it was impossible to make him blush, found himself pleasantly caught off guard. Playfully, he asked, "Would it be okay if we make it à la mode with some vanilla ice cream I purchased?"

"Hmm," I murmured, pretending to ponder for a moment before nodding in agreement. I couldn't help but wonder how a touch with something as cold and sticky as ice cream might feel—perhaps exhilarating, or maybe just a messy mistake.

Nonetheless, we ventured into the sanctuary of the bedroom, where longing whispered in the air, illuminated by the soft glow of candlelight casting shadows on the walls. Engaged in lively conversation and playful banter, our laughter intertwined with tender kisses and the sweet taste of vanilla lingering on both our lips. Time seemed to slow as we explored the depths of our connection.

As night descended, our playful banter evolved into secret declarations of love, punctuated by heated kisses and the gentle intertwining of bodies. With each tender touch, the walls between us crumbled, revealing the raw, unbridled intensity of our shared desire.

Bathed in the moon's gentle glimmer, we surrendered to the intoxicating rhythm of our love, transcending the confines of the physical world. And as fatigue finally overcame us, we found solace in each other's embrace, drifting into a peaceful slumber, cocooned in the warmth of our hard-won trust and newfound affection.

The next morning, Rico surprised me with the news that his boss had generously granted him a well-deserved day off. His boss actually had to go out of town, so there was no sense of him coming in. Eager to spend more time together, I found myself genuinely curious about Rico's plans for the day. With my schedule open and a desire to research deeper into Rico's world, I couldn't help but express my interest in joining him for whatever activities he had in mind.

"What would you be doing if I weren't here right now?" I inquired, genuinely intrigued.

Rico, always open and honest, responded without hesitation, "I'd go for a run and then hit the gym."

His suggestion resonated with me, sparking an immediate interest. "Why don't we do that together?" I proposed, feeling a sense of excitement building. "I just happen to have my gym clothes and sneakers in my car. I'll go grab them."

The suggestion struck a chord with Rico, who had always longed for a workout partner and running companion. "That's a great idea!" he exclaimed enthusiastically.

As I descended in the elevator, thoughts of Rico flooded my mind. His rugged charm, reminiscent of a man shaped by the California sun, entranced me. His sandy brown hair, adorned with highlights that gleamed like golden rays on the ocean's surface, added to his allure. Moreover, his hazel-blue eyes, tinged with a subtle touch of green, mirrored the depths of the Pacific, hinting at secrets and mysteries waiting to be uncovered.

Descending in the elevator, a wave of contentment enveloped me, a satisfied grin spreading across my face as I hurried back to my car. Retrieving my running shoes and workout bag, my mind drifted back to Rico's enigmatic allure, particularly his hands—large, powerful, and remarkably dexterous. Could their size be related to his well-endowed nature in other areas? It wasn't just their dimensions that intrigued me; it was their versatility, a testament to Rico's prowess in various pursuits, both physical and otherwise. Whether he was lifting weights at the gym or delicately handling a fine wine glass, Rico's hands exuded strength and finesse in equal measure.

As I returned to the elevator, heading back up, my mind revisited the qualities I admired most about Rico. Standing at an impressive height, his imposing figure stood tall at 6'3", adorned with a lean, muscular physique sculpted by years of disciplined fitness routines, I mused, envisioning Rico's commanding presence. His chest boasted a dusting of hair, a testament to his masculinity, leading to a tantalizing treasure trail that disappeared below his belly button, hinting at hidden delights waiting to be discovered. With each floor of the elevator ride, my aspiration to join Rico for our workout intensified, eager to experience the exhilaration of running and working out together.

I returned to the apartment carrying my workout gear, declaring, "I'll change in the bedroom, and we can hit the pavement once I'm ready."

Anticipating the run, Rico had already laced up his running shoes. While I prepared, Rico stretched his legs, readying himself for the upcoming jog.

Eagerly, we commenced our run along the River Walk, tracing a path toward the captivating lakefront.

Rico, having researched the Lakefront Trail, shared, "It's an eighteen-mile running trail, one of the most spectacular urban runs in the country." The proposed plan was to run until we collectively decided it was time to turn back.

With a playful spirit, I teased, "Let's see how far you can keep up, slowpoke!"

* * * *

Tito

Running became a shared ritual for us, and before we knew it, a month had passed by, our commitment tallying up an impressive mileage. Whether under the sun, in the rain, or even during an unexpected early snowstorm, I loved how life settled into a comforting rhythm, and the undeniable closeness between us only grew more apparent. After our run, we would work out together, share post-exercise showers, enjoy meals side by side, and, well, one gets the picture.

However, on a particular mid-October afternoon, an unexpected twist shattered the familiar pattern. After only thirty minutes, the rhythmic cadence of our run was interrupted when my Apple Watch abruptly vibrated, signaling an urgent message. A sense of foreboding loomed as I checked the notification. An emergency demanded my attention; I needed to halt running right away to call my father.

Concern etched Rico's face as he inquired, "Is everything okay?"

I felt sick, my complexion drained of color, as I replied, "Something's up. Let me give my dad a quick call."

In a sudden twist of events, I retreated to the bushes, overcome by a torrent of emotions, manifesting as heave after heave.

Alarmed, Rico pressed, "What's going on, Tito? What happened on the phone? What did your dad say?"

Wiping my face, I choked back tears as I disclosed, "My Uncle Sully was murdered. Shot seven times in a drive-by shooting, bearing all the hallmarks of a turf war with a rival mob or gang on the tough South Side of Chicago. My dad has called for an emergency meeting, and I'm not supposed to be out by myself until we gather all the details. There might be a hit out on family members; this hasn't happened in decades. Maybe my venture into selling CBD oil might have disrupted some illegal operation. Anyhow, a clear message has been sent to the Barbarotti Family."

The weight of the news struck me like a blow I couldn't ignore. "Who could have done this?" Still reeling from the revelation of Sully's murder and learning that I had to attend the family meeting, I tried my best to grapple with the gravity of the situation.

As I searched for ways to console myself, Rico suggested some stress-response techniques he learned. These techniques encompass controlled breathing, a positive mental focus, and harnessing the power of visualization. Rico emphasized the importance of nutrition in managing stress and performance, knowing that fueling my body properly was essential for both physical and mental well-being.

An air of urgency enveloped Rico as he insisted, "Your dad is right, you shouldn't be alone right now. Let's head back to my place. Once you're feeling better and rested and you've eaten something, you'll be able to think things through more clearly."

I still felt the pressure of the situation, recognizing the potential repercussions of this heinous shooting. The atmosphere was charged with the looming threat of a full-fledged gang war. In my family's current state of uncertainty, the assailants and their motives remained shrouded in mystery. Were they genuinely responding to my recent endeavors, or were these conjectures being hurled at my father by other family members?

* * * *

Rico

Amid heightened emotions, rationality took a backseat. Drawing on my psychological training, I understood the tendency of gangs to resort to immediate violence, bypassing critical thinking. I also keenly felt the weight of emotional intervention, realizing its significance for Tito, his father, and the entire Barbarotti clan.

It was imperative to inject a moment of introspection, prompting Tito and the whole Barbarotti Family to pause and assess the situation before rushing to conclusions. In essence, what everyone needed most was to take a collective step back, take deep breaths, and refrain from acting purely on the impulses of raw emotion.

Once we reached my apartment, I suggested that Tito take a long hot shower to ease his tension. As the water started flowing, I dialed Liz to share the distressing news. Recognizing the potential for heightened conflict and a potential countermove from the Barbarotti Family.

Liz promptly called me back, so I went into the living room so I couldn't be overheard. Liz started, "The FBI had not yet intervened, and the local police were still handling the situation." She continued to inform me that Lt. Guild wanted me to investigate the family's state of mind. Expressing her concerns, Liz requested "Rico please convey my condolences to Tito."

In response, I conveyed to Liz with a solemn assurance, "As I observe Tito Barbarotti in the aftermath, there's an unmistakable aura of profound hurt and sorrow permeating the air. This sudden attack has blindsided Tito and the rest of the family, thrusting them into uncharted territory."

I continued, "I aim to dig deeper into understanding his father's state of mind in the middle of this chaos. From Tito's reactions alone, it's clear that his father is grappling with a tumultuous mix of fury and anguish. They're all navigating through a fog of uncertainty, struggling to make sense of the senseless."

In all the pandemonium I tried to remain methodic and focused, "Our task now is to unearth the truth behind this heinous act. While it's premature to dredge too deeply, rest assured that I'll spare no effort in maintaining composure and gathering all pertinent details. Furthermore, I'll ensure that Tito receives your heartfelt condolences; your words of solace carry significant weight during these trying times."

I walked back into the bathroom as Tito stood under the cascading water, he was still shaken by the shocking news. Realizing that both of us needed to wash off after our run, I decided to join Tito in the shower. Moving close, I wrapped my arms around him in a tight, comforting hug. Though he was still visibly shaking, the embrace proved cathartic and provided some solace. After finishing our shower, I suggested making something to eat and advised him to contact his father for any additional information.

* * * *

Tito

As Rico started preparing scrambled eggs and toast, I dialed my dad's number. Rico overheard my voice, "I'm fine… No really, I'm okay and with Rico at his place. We were running along the Lakefront Trail when you first called me."

Rico observed me nodding in agreement, responding with phrases like "Yes, I know… Of course… Yes… I never knew that… I agree… We should reach out and talk to them." The mention of reaching out piqued Rico's interest. Once I hung up, Rico informed me that the eggs and toast were ready, prompting me to share my new information.

I shared everything with Rico, "It wasn't about me at all. Uncle Sully was involved with some group, a South Side gang called the Bad Town Faction, dealing in the illicit arms trade. Anyhow, nine members of this Bad Town Faction, a street gang, now face federal conspiracy charges in connection with an alleged gun-running operation, masterminded by three U.S. Army soldiers, that brought a host of firearms to Chicago in recent years. Uncle Sully's connection to all this remains unknown, but it wasn't sanctioned by the family, and more research needs to be done."

"Woah," exclaimed Rico, a touch of amazement in his voice. "Who were you referring to when you mentioned, 'We need to reach out and talk to them?'"

With a thoughtful look, I responded, "I meant reaching out to the rest of my family. They don't know the facts yet and might be swayed by rumors. That's why, after breakfast, I need to head to my parent's home for an emergency family meeting."

Attempting to infuse a bit of levity into the somber atmosphere, Rico quipped to me, "Well, I'd offer to meet the entire family, but given the circumstances, I guess that would be poorly timed…Just kidding!"

I raised an eyebrow in response, retorting, "Ha ha, but here's a great idea. While we have our meeting, you can go out to lunch with my mom. She's keen on meeting you."

Rico, feeling a mix of excitement and trepidation, couldn't help but wonder, "What have I gotten myself into? Are you sure it's a good idea?"

Exuding confidence, I replied, "Absolutely. She's the glue in our family. Just be your charming self, and everything will be just fine."

As they bantered back and forth, Rico's mind began to spin with thoughts of meeting my mother. He imagined scenarios ranging from awkward introductions to stalled conversations over lunch. Despite the weight of the situation, Rico found himself strangely intrigued by the prospect, eager to make a good impression on the woman who held such importance in my life. Plus, a distraction from the heavy news of Uncle Sully's demise might be just what they both needed.

The idea of meeting my extended family sparked a sense of curiosity within Rico. He had heard stories about the colorful characters that made up my Barbarotti clan, tales of eccentric uncles, spirited aunts, and cousins with nicknames like "Vinny the Nutcracker" and "Ronnie Stained Grin." While the circumstances surrounding their meeting were far from ideal, Rico couldn't deny the allure of being drawn into my vibrant family dynamic.

With a wry smile, I imagined Rico navigating the intricate social dynamics of my family gatherings, trying to find his place among the boisterous laughter and affectionate jibes. It was a far cry from his family gatherings, which he told me tended to be more subdued and conventional affairs filled with polite conversation and obligatory pleasantries. But Rico was nothing if not adaptable, and he welcomed the opportunity to immerse himself in my world, however crazy and offbeat it might be.

CHAPTER 5

Tito

Rico and I cruised down the road toward the Barbarotti residence—the house I grew up in. Nestled against Lincoln Park, it had evolved from a modest abode to a magnificent mansion over the years, maintaining its historical charm while integrating modern conveniences. Dating back to the early 1900s, the structure underwent meticulous renovations, eventually earning recognition as a historical landmark in 2016. However, during my youth, it was still a work in progress, far from the beauty it embodies today.

As we arrived, Rico stood there, feeling like a deer caught in the headlights of an oncoming mobster Cadillac. He couldn't help but question his life choices. The estate's grandeur now overshadowed the impending encounter with my formidable mom.

I flashed a grin as wide as a mafia don's ledger of debts, and reassured Rico, "Just be yourself, Rico. Today, you probably won't meet my dad, but my mom, Virginia, is eager to get to know you. She's already planned something impressive, no doubt. You're going to just love her, trust me!"

As we stepped through the back entrance, the kitchen greeted us with a whirlwind of activity, reminiscent of a bustling paparazzi swarm. The Barbarotti Family members, bound by blood or loyalty, filled the room, some with roots so deep in the family that they practically had their own branch on the family tree.

Surrounded by the kitchen madness, Virginia, the matriarch, stood like a mob queen among the hanging pots and pans. Dressed in what could only be described as "mob wife chic," she was a vision of ostentatious elegance, making minimalist 2023 decor cower in shame. White and black checkered floors set the stage for a classy aesthetic, a far cry from restrained minimalism.

Virginia's presence, larger than life, radiated authenticity and authority. Her smile, more a subtle menace than a welcoming gesture, and the glimmer in her eye as she appraised Rico from head to toe, hinted at the intricate dance of power and charm that defined her world.

"Okay, now I get it!" Virginia said, "You are definitely one tall glass of water, Mr. Baas. Hmm, I look forward to getting to know you better, even though I feel I already know all about you," she deliberately slowly said each word drawled from her southern roots, elongating the word "all" like a suspenseful pause in a sitcom.

Closing the kitchen door with a theatrical flair that would make a Broadway diva jealous, she continued with a mischievous glint in her eye, "Now that I have your undivided attention, we'll let Tito go to the 'Family Meeting,' while you, Rico, and I embark on a secret rendezvous."

The words hung in the air, leaving Rico feeling like the main character in a botched mob plan. After all, nothing says "mob family introduction" like a secret rendezvous with the mob mom.

* * * *

Rico

I discovered that I didn't have to drive Tito's Tesla and breathed a sigh of relief as I quipped, "I'm grateful that I'm not being entrusted with the task of navigating a car equipped with more gadgets than a spaceship—a vehicle that seemed to demand a pilot's license." Luckily, the universe had smiled upon me, and "Lady Virginia" had her own chauffeur named James, ferrying us towards our next adventure.

With an air of sophistication that could rival a queen's decree, Virginia leaned towards the driver, proclaiming, "To the Waldorf Astoria Spa, my good sir! We shall be pampered and attended to with the utmost care, as is our due."

Her orders set the course for a rendezvous with luxury. "Afterwards, we will amble over to the Brass Tack, nestled within the Waldorf Astoria, to enjoy their impressive menu featuring American cuisine that shall no doubt serenade our palates. James, you can pick us up in about three hours but call me first to make sure. Rico, my dear, does this plan tickle your fancy?" Virginia inquired, her eyes twinkling with a playful charm.

I, already bowled over by the unfolding spectacle, responded with unfeigned admiration, "Impressed doesn't even begin to cover it. You could suggest McDonald's, and I'm certain you'd make it feel like the Ritz Carlton."

Virginia beamed, her smile radiant, "Smooth as silk, Rico. I predict we're going to hit it off famously!"

In the sleek confines of the chauffeured vehicle, I ditched the formalities and opted for a casual chat with Virginia. "Mrs. Barbarotti," I began with a directness befitting the gravity of our circumstances, "We both acknowledge the intricacies of the situation at hand. As a criminal psychology expert, my top priority is preventing an escalation to a retaliatory attack or gang war.

Now, changing the subject, I hold a genuine affinity for your son, Tito, and I believe he reciprocates those feelings. His aspirations to transform the business into a legitimate venture resonate with me, and I find myself wondering about my role in all of this, from your perspective."

Virginia, her gaze steady and her demeanor composed, responded with a calm authority. "First and foremost, Rico, please, call me Virginia. I hope it's acceptable for me to address you as Rico."

I nodded in agreement.

Virginia continued, "Now, Rico, I've been the mediator between my husband and son for quite some time. I discerned Tito's truth about his sexuality before he did, and I've been instrumental in nudging my husband toward acceptance. However, the broader family dynamic is more complex. Tito's charisma and honesty have garnered him numerous admirers, but, as you well know, there are those who may exploit perceived weaknesses. Having grown up in the mob milieu, I understand the barbarous nature of this business—literally and figuratively. Let me be unequivocal: I am committed to ensuring the safety of my family. I'm assisting Tito in adopting a legitimate approach. We aim to navigate within the bounds of the legal system, but we won't bow down to intimidation. Self-defense, Rico, falls well within those legal boundaries."

I absorbed Virginia's insights; my responses were measured and deliberate. "I grasp the concept of self-defense as well, Virginia. Drawing a line between protecting oneself in the moment and seeking retribution afterward is crucial. I'm here to help if I can, to figure out those responsible for Uncle Sully's murder. Regardless of their involvement in questionable activities, a drive-by shooting is unacceptable under any circumstances. Too many young lives are lost to such senseless violence, and I'm committed to putting an end to it."

Virginia, her demeanor retaining its composed grace, reassured me, "Rico, we're aligned in our perspective. Based on the evidence gathered by other family members, it appears to be an isolated incident involving the Bad Town Faction. Sully happened to be in the wrong place at the wrong time. He wasn't directly tied to the gun-running operations but was providing information to dissuade the guns from entering our territory. We share your concern about youth violence, but our influence doesn't extend to the South Side. Sully's situation is, unfortunately, a matter of adverse circumstances."

Virginia continued, "Now, I requested Tito to bring you here so I could finally meet you face-to-face. He can't stop talking about you, and I've never seen him so invested in someone before. There's something special between you two, and my intention is to help you comprehend our family dynamics and the intricacies of the family business. I'm here to address any queries you might have, hoping you realize that, someday, you could become part of our family. In the grand tradition of parental interrogations, let's cut to the chase: spill the beans, Rico—what are your true intentions?"

In a burst of earnestness and a touch of humor, I replied, "Well, my intentions are to get to know Tito and his family as well as I can because I plan on spending a great deal of time with him. I can honestly tell you he is the first man I have ever dated seriously, and I'm trying to do my best to keep him around!"

Virginia warmly grabbed my hand, a tear glistening in her eye, as she said, "You realize that falling in love with Tito means you will also fall in love with his whole family and vice versa. We are very old school, and now that marriage equality is legal, we hope that you both will make a legal man of our boy Tito!"

I was pleasantly surprised by Virginia's acceptance and progressiveness of our relationship. However, I couldn't help but wonder if Tito's father would be equally open and accepting.

Sensing my unspoken thoughts, Virginia added, "Now, there will be a significant service for Rico's Uncle Sully, but I don't want that to be your first exposure to the entire Barbarotti Family. Would you please consider coming over this Sunday for one of our annual dinners? This way, you can meet everyone in a more relaxed social setting, and they can get to know you. Get ready for a classic Italian razzing or hazing, as some like to put it. It's all part of our tradition, and I trust you can handle it. From what I've seen, you navigate everything with grace. I'm usually one with a perfect record of spotting someone with great character, and you've checked all the right boxes!"

The limo glided to a halt at the Waldorf, and Virginia chimed in, "You don't have to answer this second, but chew it over while we get a mani and a pedi and a relaxing massage. After the week we've both been through, we deserve it!"

I, a bit sheepish, admitted, "I don't know what a mani and a pedi are because I've never had one, neither a massage, but I guess I'll find out."

Virginia sported a mischievous grin, "Well, you're in for a slice of heaven, a piece of paradise, and a bundle of joy all rolled into one! You won't believe what you've been missing! Consider it a crash course in the art of pampering, Rico!"

Before you knew it, I was sprawled in a reclining chair, sporting a cucumber mask on my face and cucumber slices gracefully perched on my eyes for that refreshing, natural lift. A skilled manicurist diligently tended to my hands, providing an extra dose of luxury with a sea salt massage and a follow-up hot wax treatment. Simultaneously, a dedicated foot specialist lavished the same royal treatment on my feet. Picture the finale—my legs, basking in the sea salt scrub, receive a soothing massage, while my feet, one at a time, luxuriate in a hot wax bath. As I melted into the massage chair, now expertly set to Swedish tapping mode, I attempted to express my bliss, but the words stuttered out in a shaky, near-seizure fashion. In reality, I was far from convulsing—I was in a state of pure Shangri-La.

If only Tito could witness this spectacle, he'd be the one convulsing... with laughter. Unbeknownst to me, Virginia couldn't resist capturing this blissful moment on her phone, figuring the video might come in handy for some light-hearted blackmail if the need arises. After all, every pampered moment deserves its place in the family album!

The extravagant spoiling session extended beyond expectations, leaving Virginia ravenously hungry and determined not to linger any longer when it came to lunch. "Well, Rico," Virginia quipped, "How did your little pampering feel?"

I, basking in the afterglow of my spa escapade, grinned and replied, "I feel like a new man; my arms and legs are ready to float away."

"Well, I don't know about you, but I'm famished for lunch. Let's make our way over to Brass Tack's; they feature impressive American cuisine highlighting the freshest and finest ingredients! A touch of pampering followed by a dash of culinary delight—the perfect prescription for a day well spent, don't you agree?"

Virginia and I had just settled into our seats when Tito rang my phone to let him know that the Family Meeting was over. I asked him how it went, which piqued Virginia's curiosity as well. She suggested putting Tito on speaker, but I replied, "Not here … not a good idea … I'll fill you in, in a minute. Excuse me."

I walked to an area of the restaurant where there were no people, to talk in confidence. I asked Tito, "So, it didn't go as well as you thought? What happened?"

Tito explained, "Well, Sully did get ambushed, but it happened because he was in a place he shouldn't have been from the start. However, there is no worry of retaliation. There's no revenge plot or anything like that. Every single member agreed it was an unfortunate blunder with Uncle Sully being in the wrong place at the wrong time. However, the Bad Town Faction will be making an appearance at the funeral, trying to make amends for the shooting. But what rubbed me the wrong way, was that many in the Family don't think this is a good time for me to take control, and they feel I lack the old-school approach needed to lead."

I responded to Tito, "Maybe they're onto something with the old-school approach to dealing with the old gang. That's the problem—they're stuck in an antique business model, and that's their only playbook. You've got fantastic ideas, Tito, but you need fresh young minds like yours to breathe life into them. You've inherited your father's connections and his well-established distribution channels, but you don't need your father's cronies, who oppose your leadership, blocking your path. Forge your own way. What is it that you truly want to achieve in your heart? You've expressed a desire to legitimize the Family Business, once synonymous with organized crime, and transform it into a successful, organized business venture … So, let's make it happen! Establish a separate wing or division and bring your vision to fruition. I'm here to assist you, and together, we'll assemble the right team for the job!"

Tito absorbed my words, wrestling with the conflicting demands of family loyalty and personal aspirations. His father's expectations loomed large, emphasizing the importance of allegiance that held the family together.

Trying to convey this to me, Tito was met with a straightforward response: "Don't put your life on hold to please everyone but yourself, and don't let misguided loyalty lead you into breaking the law for others' gain."

My words lingered, leaving Tito with much to contemplate. Nevertheless, he maintained a cheerful facade in front of the Family, bidding me a pleasant lunch with his mom and sending his regards. Expressing a touch of envy for our spa time and one of his favorite lunch spots, Tito yearned for the shared experience. I assured him that the enjoyment would be far greater with his company, but Virginia was ensuring I was well taken care of in his absence.

I rejoined Virginia at the table, aware of the anticipation hanging in the air. Choosing my words carefully, I began, "The meeting went well in terms of preventing any immediate retaliation or revenge for Sully's death. It does appear to have been a case of mistaken identity. The culprits are already in custody, and members of the Bad Town Faction are coming to pay their respects at the funeral, collaborating with the Family to make amends."

Virginia, ever perceptive, interjected, "But you mentioned it didn't go as well as expected, or something of the sort."

I noted Virginia's acute hearing and answered, "That was in reference to Tito taking over the reins. Some Family members either think it's not the right time or doubt Tito's capabilities."

Virginia stood up for her son, stating emphatically, "Tito has precisely what it takes to propel the Barbarotti Family into the 21st century. He brings fresh ideas and strategies to keep us out of trouble."

I, unable to hold back, added, "But you can't teach old dog new tricks. To build a new, younger organization, you need new blood."

The term resonated with Virginia, prompting her to argue, "We don't have relationships with these so-called 'younger thinking minds.' How can we trust them?"

In Tito's defense, I responded, "Like any CEO, you pick your best people and build trust through leadership, and Tito has the charisma, intelligence, innovation, and progressive thinking needed for a winning business model in today's corporate landscape."

Virginia, sensing the weight of my words, decided to shift the focus, saying, "How about we just order lunch and enjoy it until we can all get together later to discuss these ideas."

Aware that convincing Salvador might require divine intervention, Virginia acknowledged the challenge. In Salvador's mind, Tito would follow in his footsteps, continuing the legacy he had built. While the notion of Tito becoming a mob kingpin might be a stretch, it echoed an age-old familial dilemma—parents grappling with their children's aspirations versus the desire to mold them into replicas of themselves.

I remembered studying situations like this in his psychology group. "Normally, young people rebel to be independent, either by doing their own thing or trying to get their parents to back them up. The studies showed that rebellion, which we usually think of as seeking independence, is actually a way of showing dependence."

I thought that letting Tito start his own part of the family business wouldn't just be good for the family but would also make Tito feel like he really belonged. I also genuinely felt that allowing Tito to navigate the consequences of his choices would lead to success. In my heart, I knew Tito possessed the qualities necessary to triumph.

As thoughts swirled through my mind, I decided it might be wise to listen to Virginia and shift my focus to lunch. When our server finally arrived to take our order, it was evident that he was either frustrated, upset, or both. While it's understandable to have a bad day, it's another matter to project those issues onto the customers you're supposed to serve. Virginia, not one to let anyone dampen her spirits on her spa day and lunch, rolled her eyes in disapproval.

I commented, "I guess everyone is entitled to have a bad day," attempting to diffuse the tension.

However, Virginia, determined to maintain the positive atmosphere, countered, "Well, that may be true, but this guy is upset because he had to work breakfast and now lunch, and he hasn't had a break since he got here at six A.M. to prep this morning. But why is that our problem?"

In the background, we could hear shouting, "I don't care. I've been here since early this morning, and I need to take a break and eat something."

A manager's voice attempted to reason, "Just finish up lunch, and I'll give you an hour lunch break."

The server, losing patience, screamed, "Forget it. I'm not waiting two hours until I get a break. Screw it, I QUIT!"

Observing the scene, I turned to Virginia and suggested, "Do you just want to order takeout and bring it home to eat?"

Virginia, appreciating the idea, responded, "That's a wonderful idea. Let's order now, and I can get something for Tito as well. This has never happened before; I'm so sorry."

"Please, this isn't your fault." I reassured her, "Things like this happen all the time, and it isn't going to ruin our spa high."

Virginia smiled and said, "Come here, Rico. Let's share a hearty hug and turn this lunch fiasco into a homey feast at home. Who needs a grumpy server when we've got each other, both massaged, pampered, and ready for a cozy dining experience in familiar surroundings with Tito, who will surely brighten up both of our days."

In a twist of fate, as I finalized my takeout order with Virginia, my phone buzzed with a work call. "I need to take this outside, sorry," I said, slipping out the front door.

Answering the call, I heard Lieutenant Guild's voice on the other end. "Hello, Lieutenant Guild. Is everything okay?" I inquired. The response wasn't what he expected.

"Well, Rico, the supposed report by the local authorities regarding Sully Barbarotti's incident, claiming it was an open-and-shut case of a drive-by hitting the wrong person, isn't as straightforward as it seemed."

Intrigued, I asked, "Who was the intended person supposed to be?"

"That's a good question," Lieutenant Guild replied. "But don't say anything to Tito yet. We believe Sully Barbarotti might not be the sole target, and the Bad Town Faction, a heavily armed black gang, may have ambitions beyond controlling the South Side. New intel suggests they could be eyeing the North Side, with potential plans to take over the Barbarotti Family's territory. This isn't confirmed yet, so keep it under wraps. I want you to stay alert in undercover mode when you're around them. Stay alert for any mention of the Bad Town Faction attending Sully's funeral. Do you have details on who and when this is happening?"

I responded, "I don't. The Barbarotti Family just wrapped up their meeting, convinced it was a case of mistaken identity. They believe the Bad Town Faction is coming in good faith to make amends at the funeral. But Lieutenant, something doesn't smell right to me."

My mind buzzed with questions. "Why would the Bad Town Faction, or the BTF group as he prefers to call them, be involved in pilfering and smuggling over ninety guns along with tons of ammunition brought in by gun runners from Tennessee? What's their endgame, and what did Tito's Uncle Sully know that might have cost him his life?" The revelation sent a shiver down my spine, raising ominous thoughts.

A foreboding feeling gripped me as I pondered the possibilities. Was the BTF planning something more sinister, and did Uncle Sully stumble upon a dangerous secret? I couldn't shake my intuition that the Barbarotti Family, including Salvador, Virginia, and Tito, might be in jeopardy. Keeping a composed exterior, I knew I needed to be on high alert. A quick detour to my place to retrieve my concealed firearm was on the agenda. In the face of uncertainty, I was determined to safeguard not just my own life but also that of my beloved Tito and my newfound extended family.

As Virginia and I were preparing to make an exit, a fellow family member's wife named Pam, a petite and charming middle-aged woman, approached us.

Dressed elegantly, she couldn't help but express concern, "You two rushing off and not enjoying your meal in such a nice place?"

Virginia, ever the diplomat, responded, "Oh, too much drama going on here today. We thought we'd join up with Tito at home and bring him a treat since the meeting is already over."

Pam, with a hint of shock in her eyes, chimed in, "It was so startling to hear about Sully. You know, my Vinny and Sully basically grew up together, even though they were cousins. Anyhow, Vinny told me that Sully was acting very weird the past few weeks, and he wondered if something might be wrong …maybe money problems?"

Seizing the opportunity to gather more information, I introduced myself: "Hello, Pam. I'm Rico, a close friend of Tito's. Did your husband ever mention if Sully was involved in any business dealings on the South Side of Chicago?"

Pam hesitated for a moment but then replied, "I'm sorry, did you and Tito go to school together? Is that how you know each other?"

I, being upfront, confessed, "No, actually, we are currently dating, and Tito was wondering why Sully would be mixed up with any gang activity on the South Side."

Pam disclosed, "Well, my husband mentioned Sully knew some loan sharks that dealt on the South Side, but I'm not sure if it had anything to do with him at all."

Sensing the direction of my questioning, Virginia gracefully intervened, "Well, Pam, we don't want our lunch to get cold, so we'll get in touch later, and I'll bring you up to speed on all I've heard as well."

Pam bid them farewell, and Virginia led me towards the waiting limo with James, bound for home.

On the way back, I casually suggested a quick stop at my apartment building, citing a forgotten work-related matter—an essential letter that urgently needed to be mailed. Unbeknownst to Virginia, my primary mission was to retrieve my trusty sidekick, the Glock Nineteen.

I felt secure knowing I had all the necessary clearances to carry it undercover during emergencies. I deemed the recent developments concerning Tito and his family as a pressing concern. As a top-notch marksman in my graduating class, I had not only demonstrated unparalleled intelligence but also exhibited exceptional aim, breaking target accuracy records that even the FBI found remarkable.

I also understood that FBI agents are mandated to keep our firearms on hand during duty hours and specific off-duty circumstances. This policy ensures preparedness and quick response to unforeseen challenges.

In a swift move, I slipped an envelope into the mailbox, maintaining an air of secrecy about my mission, and we promptly headed to the Barbarotti Estate.

CHAPTER 6

Tito

After the family meeting had concluded, I entered the kitchen and was pleasantly surprised to find my mom and Rico already at home.

My mom declared, "No need to worry about lunch preparations—we brought your favorite Brass Tack burger."

Intrigued, I asked, "Why the change of plans? Why dine at home instead of the restaurant?"

Virginia, unpacking a well-prepared bag, explained, "In short, dear, too much drama with the staff, and we figured there's no better company than yours for a meal!"

A wide grin spread across my face as I exclaimed, "What a pleasant surprise! I was just craving a B.T. Burger with Butterkase cheese and griddled onions. It's like you read my mind!"

Rico joined in, "Your mom convinced me that it's your absolute favorite, so I had to give it a try myself. Now we can be burger buddies."

In strolled my father, Salvador Senior, a figure larger than life, the grand puppeteer orchestrating the unseen threads of the Barbarotti legacy. His professional alias, Greasy Hand Salv, required no introduction; his commanding presence filled the room, defying the stereotypical image of an Italian mobster. My dad's broad shoulders carried the weight of authority, adorned in a tailored suit that spoke of affluence rather than underworld affiliations. His eyes, sharp and penetrating, bore the tales of a lifetime spent navigating treacherous waters.

Far from the stereotypical mobster, my father had salt-and-pepper hair framed a face etched with experiences that transcended the confines of organized crime. A meticulously groomed beard added an air of sophistication, and his hands, paradoxically, were immaculately clean. The moniker Greasy Hand Salv, whispered in hushed tones, only served to deepen the enigma surrounding him.

But for right now he was just my dad, entering with a commanding presence, a stride that echoed authority without the need for words. He wasted no time with pleasantries, his voice a low, rumbling symphony that demanded attention. "Couldn't resist coming back for more, could you, honey?" The words, laced with a peculiar blend of charm and danger, revealed the complexity within the man.

Mom acknowledged his entrance with an indulgent smile, her eyes reflecting a history of shared endeavors. "You're always my destination, my dear. Oh, let me introduce you to someone. This is Mr. Rico Baas, the young man who's been occupying our son's free time lately."

Salvador, or Sal as I and the immediate family affectionately addressed my father, fixed his gaze upon Rico, a discerning look that seemed to peel away layers.

Sal's voice, a loud whisper reminiscent of the Godfather delivering a mob order, cut through the air, "Well, young man, it's about time you finally showed your face. I was starting to think Tito made you up." The remark, wrapped in a cloak of wry amusement, concealed the shrewdness beneath Sal's façade.

As Rico navigated the intensity of his gaze, he couldn't help but feel that my father was a mosaic of contradictions, a character painted with hues that transcended the stark black and white of organized crime lore. At that moment, the room seemed to hold its breath, as if Sal's words lingered in the air, carrying an unspoken weight that added an extra layer to the mystery of the Barbarotti Family.

Rico approached, extended his hand, and replied, "It's a pleasure to meet you, Mr. Barbarotti. I assure you, I'm very real and thoroughly enjoy my time with your son. I hope that's all right to say."

Dad chuckled, "Of course, it's all right. Please, call me Sal. We've heard so much about you; it feels like you're already family."

Rico marveled at Sal's warmth and wondered whether it was genuine or a front for his benefit. It seemed sincere, but Rico wasn't sure. All he knew was that he wanted to share with Sal the potential dangers of a gang war.

My dad excused himself, adding, "Don't let me interrupt your meal. I have a lunch meeting to attend to myself. Nice meeting you, Rico."

He went to kiss Mom and me as she reminded him, "Don't forget, we're meeting Sully's widow, Maxine, tonight. I'm having lunch with her two sons tomorrow; call me later if you need anything. Love you, honey!"

For now, our focus was on savoring lunch while Rico felt a swell of pride and apprehension as he pondered that my father already knew of him. The realization that his own parents remained in the dark about his relationship with me sparked a twinge of guilt. Rico confided in me that he couldn't help but wonder how his parents would react to the news of our relationship, especially considering their conservative views.

The thought of revealing not only our relationship but also my family's background, including my father's ties to the Mafia, stirred a sense of unease. Yet, I reassured him that he could address his concerns in due time, perhaps during their next phone call. After all, there were more immediate matters at hand, such as navigating the complexities of my family for now.

As the three of us settled around the kitchen nook table, we eagerly dug into our lunches. Virginia, breaking the delightful silence, announced, "Tito, I've invited Rico to join us for our Family dinner this Sunday. Considering it is just two days before Halloween, I thought we could turn it into a festive Halloween Party. What do you think?"

I paused between bites, responding, "Mom, I'm not sure. With the funeral arrangements still pending, should we be planning a party?" Virginia countered, "Why not focus on something that brings the family together in joy rather than being overwhelmed by sadness? Sully loved Halloween, and I know his sons and his wife enjoyed it, too. Let's celebrate his life instead of mourning it. What's your take, Rico?"

* * * *

Rico

I, wiping sauce from my burger, contemplated, "Um, well, Halloween will happen regardless, and it's one of my favorite times to celebrate…as long as it's done tastefully and respectfully. I think it could be fun, but then again, this would be my first gathering with your entire family. It's a bit of a toss-up, I suppose."

Tito couldn't help but voice his internal conflict, asking, "So, any idea when they plan to hold the funeral?"

Virginia, with a poised yet compassionate demeanor, responded, "Your father is in talks with Aunt Maxine as we speak. They're leaning towards the second week of November, specifically Wednesday, the 8th. They've already cremated Uncle Sully, so an open casket isn't an option. Let's set aside mourning for November 8th. This family deserves a respite from grief, a moment of distraction. I'll reach out to Maxine to ensure she's comfortable with the idea, making sure it doesn't strike any dissonant chords."

After a moment of reflection, Tito agreed, "All right, I'm on board with this, but it's crucial that Aunt Maxine and Rico are in agreement."

I, radiating enthusiasm, chimed in, "Well, I've orchestrated some legendary Halloween bashes back in California, so why not make a grand entrance here in Chicago? I'm in, and with your mom's blond locks, we just need a wig for your dad, and voila! Barbie and Ken, mob style?" With a playful grin, Rico continued, "As for us, what about two dashing pirates?"

"Imagine my dad trying to pull off the Ken look!" Tito erupted into laughter, envisioning the improbable sight of my dad as Ken. Suggestively, Tito proposed, "Alternatively, how about Batman and Robin for us? However, we'd need to determine our roles. Given my younger age, I'll assume the Robin persona. What do you think?"

Engulfed in infectious laughter, I exclaimed, "Oh, the possibilities are endless—let's dive in and make it unforgettable!"

With Maxine's approval in hand, Virginia embarked on a mission against time, orchestrating a Halloween extravaganza with mere days to spare. Tito and I plunged into the digital abyss, scouring the web for elusive costume options. Meanwhile, Virginia, relieved of the task of sending formal invitations to the tight-knit clan, found herself dialing numbers, ensuring everyone was in the loop about the costume party—with a strict embargo on mobster attire.

The chosen theme? Silver screen icons. My initial visions of caped crusaders or swashbuckling pirates hit a snag as popular outfits flew off the shelves. Undeterred, Tito proposed a new concept: "Men in Black." A sleek ensemble featuring a noir suit, crisp white shirt, and the quintessential Ray-Ban Predator 2 Sunglasses, accompanied by a Series 4 De-Atomizers, promised to repel any potential extraterrestrial interlopers.

While Tito reveled in the creative surge, a sense of vigilance lingered, a constant reminder of the looming threat posed by the BTF. They cast a shadow over the festive preparations, even though we tried to put Uncle Sully's farewell at the back of our minds.

Tito and his mom started brainstorming some decoration ideas as I stepped outside to make a work phone call.

I called Lieutenant Guild to inform him about his first face-to-face meeting with Salvador Barbarotti Senior and to let him know about the forthcoming Halloween party where I would have an opportunity to engage with the entire Barbarotti Family. The Lieutenant expressed his excitement over my progress in building connections within the family but remained focused on the urgency and diligence needed, considering the potential threat from the BTF.

I inquired about the involvement of undercover agents within the Southside gang and sought any inside information they might have gathered. The Lieutenant shared it was an ongoing investigation with third party affiliations, lacking specific timelines or explicit targets.

Lieutenant Guild emphasized, "The validity and urgency of the information, was convinced that an attack wasn't merely a possibility but an imminent threat. With a small and guarded group like the BTF, all outsiders were viewed as potential threats."

I heightened my vigilance, and before long, the party materialized as if it had been meticulously planned for weeks. Opting for catering, Virginia aimed to focus on her costume and hosting duties. As Sunday dawned, the weather turned blustery with showers, a crisp forty-six degrees marking the fleeting high temperature.

Unfortunately, Tito caught wind of the weather report, and the mercury was set to plummet to thirty-six degrees in the evening with heavier showers. Undeterred, Tito and I returned from the Halloween Party Store with bags brimming with decorations. Together, the three of us transformed the interior of the house into a Halloween spectacle, adorned with cobwebs, bats, witches, spiders, and all things eerie.

* * * *

Tito

Rico and I also pitched in, adorning the space with stark uplighting on scary dummies from a Halloween store, creating an ambiance reminiscent of the Addams Family house. It seemed fitting, considering Virginia and Sal embraced their roles as Morticia and Gomez, channeling the inner Catherine Zeta-Jones and Luis Guzmán versions from the popular "Wednesday" TV series. Uncannily resembling their on-screen counterparts, everything fell into place, leaving Rico in awe of the setup. However, I knew that my mother's touch would undoubtedly make it one memorable party!

The stage was set, awaiting the arrival of the esteemed Family guests. Rico and I hurried up to my childhood haven, ready to transform into our Men in Black personas. It was Rico's inaugural exploration of the entire house, and his first time stepping into my sacred space that held all my memories.

The room struck Rico with awe at its meticulous organization. My awards adorned the walls like an illustrious tapestry, and a dresser drawer with shelves above displayed a symphony of my trophies—from tennis triumphs to running feats, and speech contests to scholarships. My room had become a shrine thanks to my mother; she organized everything as a testament to the overachievements of a young man determined to leave an indelible mark on the world.

As the clock struck six P.M., party time, a tidal wave of guests flooded in, each adding to the bustling sea of people. Rico, caught in the surge of newcomers, couldn't help but voice his curiosity. "How extensive is your family, Tito? Are these predominantly blood relatives, or are we expecting a mix of in-laws and neighbors, too?"

I, adjusting my sleek *Men in Black* costume, chuckled before diving into the intricate family tree. "Well, brace yourself. My dad is the second oldest among sixteen siblings, including two sets of twins. On my mom's side, she has ten siblings. So, technically, everyone gracing us with their presence today is a blood relative or their spouse. I have a whopping fifty-four first cousins from my dad's side and ten from my mom's side. Imagine having sixty-four kids at your birthday parties when you were young—I know, I was spoiled rotten!"

Rico, clad in his black suit and dark sunglasses, stood there, jaw agape, absorbing the staggering familial statistics. "Unbelievable. Your grandmother probably relocated just to avoid more pregnancies."

I had to laugh, thinking that my grandmother probably would have done anything to avoid getting pregnant again after having seventeen kids. Remembering every face wasn't a Herculean task for me, but for Rico, it would definitely take a while. With graceful charm, I began greeting each person as they entered.

"Hello Uncle Vinny and Aunt Pam," Rico acknowledged Pam, evoking the memory of their recent encounter at Brass Tacks.

I effortlessly recognized every person, even beneath their costumes—Uncle Al, Uncle Joey, Uncle Bob, Uncle Patrick, Uncle Danny, and the list kept on going. The room transformed into a lively spectacle, featuring monsters, and believe it or not, there ended up being a couple portraying Barbie and Ken. There was one standout duo as Clarice Starling played by Jody Foster wheeling in Hannibal Lecter portrayed by Anthony Hopkins from *"The Silence of the Lambs."* It became a mesmerizing blend of Hollywood characters, some easily identifiable, while others demanded a touch of guesswork. The entire gathering unfolded as a last-minute Halloween party, conjured up with delightful spontaneity.

* * * *

Rico

I kept a watchful eye on Tito, as we stayed close to the comforting presence of Morticia and Gomez, Tito's parents. However, a chance encounter with one of Tito's uncles, the infamous Ron or Ronnie Stained Grin, proved to be less than pleasant. I was immediately struck by Ronnie's unkempt appearance—an unsettling combination of nicotine-stained teeth, a protruding beer gut, and greasy, unkempt hair. Ronnie's attire, resembling that of a downtrodden vagrant, made it difficult to discern whether he was in costume or simply living his everyday life.

As Ronnie unleashed a barrage of homophobic remarks directed at Tito and me, something about a sissy boy taking over the organization. I couldn't help but notice the pungent odor emanating from his breath, a stark reminder of his disregard for personal hygiene. Reflecting on the encounter, I realized that Ronnie was the family's perennial black sheep—a troubled man burdened by a history of abusive behavior towards his wife, frequent encounters with law enforcement for public intoxication and domestic violence, and a lengthy rap sheet adorned with DUI charges.

Tito cautioned me to avoid the toxic individual, likening Ronnie to the mercury in a thermometer. Some family members radiate warmth while others, like Ronnie, exude a chilling coldness.

I nodded in understanding, sharing my own familial anecdotes of bigotry and unpleasant relatives, including my uncle, Johan, from my father's side, whose presence at holiday gatherings was always a source of discomfort. "There's always that one uncle you wish would skip the family dinners," I remarked, empathizing with Tito's predicament.

The remainder of the evening unfolded with warmth and camaraderie enveloping me bounded by the Barbarotti clan. I found myself in the company of Sully's widow, Maxine, a woman whose resilience shone through even in the face of grief.

Maxine, standing at a petite five feet four inches, with chestnut-brown hair streaked with hints of silver, greeted me with a warm smile. Her brown eyes, framed by delicate laugh lines, exuded kindness, and wisdom. Despite her petite frame, she emanated strength, a quality evident in the way she held herself with poise and grace.

I paid my respects to her and inquired about attending the funeral services, expressing my desire to support Tito and his newfound family bond. Maxine's gracious response was immediate, welcoming me with open arms and affirming her appreciation for my presence in Tito's life. She spoke fondly of Tito, hailing that he was her favorite nephew, a beacon of support in times of need, especially now that Sully was gone. As Maxine recounted cherished memories of her late husband, tears welled up in her eyes, revealing the depth of her love and loss.

I, ever the gentleman, offered my handkerchief, a small gesture of comfort amid sorrow. Our conversation explored deeper, touching upon family dynamics and the importance of positive role models. Empathetic and genuine, I expressed my eagerness to connect with Maxine and her sons, recognizing the significance of familial bonds in times of loss. Maxine, moved by my kindness, saw in me the same warmth and humor that endeared Tito to her heart. She sensed she had made a new friend, and so did I.

* * * *

Tito

The vivid scene unfolded amidst the swirling throng of costumed revelers, where my vivacious cousin Cheryl, sporting a rebellious streak of green in her bleach-white hair, bore a striking resemblance to the music sensation Billie Eilish.

Her words carried a playful edge, reminiscing about my past allure as the enigmatic heartthrob, surrounded by female admirers enchanted by my magnetic charm.

Now, as I embrace my newfound authenticity, I offered a glimpse into my inner journey, shedding the cloak of pretense to reveal my true self. Our exchange was infused with sincerity, each word a testament to the path of self-discovery.

In the middle of the lively banter, Cheryl playfully likened her quest for companionship to a fishing expedition, in search of that elusive catch.

I simply smiled, radiating contentment, as I acknowledged, "I've already found mine," highlighting the serendipitous nature of my newfound love. With a nod to fate, I bid Cheryl farewell, eager to return to the side of my beloved, leaving the gaiety of the party to unfold. How I loved using the word gaiety in a non-gay manner. LOL.

As the evening's festivities drew to a close and the clock approached eleven P.M., Rico felt the weight of impending responsibilities pressing on his mind, a reminder of the duties awaiting him at dawn. Despite lingering uncertainty about whether I would be comfortable with his departure, Rico's primary concern remained the safety of my family.

I assured Rico that I understood his need for a good night's sleep and pledged to remain vigilant, keeping my attention focused on any potential threats looming over the Barbarotti clan, but I knew my dad had people guarding the property as well.

As the night came to a close, Rico approached my parents with gratitude and warmth to bid farewell and express his appreciation for the delightful evening. Despite his regret at having to depart early due to a morning work commitment, Rico conveyed his sincere gratitude for their hospitality and the opportunity to meet some of their extended family.

Virginia graciously dismissed his concerns about helping with cleanup, praising his contributions to the festivities alongside mine. "I hope our family didn't overwhelm you," Virginia remarked with a smile, acknowledging the boisterous nature of both sides of our combined families.

Rico reciprocated the sentiment, praising their hospitality and expressing his fondness for everyone present, save perhaps for Uncle Ronnie. "This evening has been simply charming," he declared, "And both you and Sal have been such hospitable hosts."

Virginia and Sal shared a chuckle at Rico's mention of Uncle Ronnie, with Sal offering a resigned quip about the complexities of family dynamics. "Well, sorry about Ronnie," he conceded, "he's a pain in the ass, but what can you do, it's Familia!"

CHAPTER 7

Rico

As I made my way home from the party, the prospect of an early morning briefing loomed large in my mind. This briefing represented a crucial opportunity to dig deeper into the activities of the Bad Town Faction, offering a potential breakthrough in understanding the circumstances surrounding Sully's tragic demise.

While anticipating clarity, I couldn't shake a nagging suspicion regarding the BTFs sudden display of condolences to the Barbarotti Family. Their gestures felt disingenuous, raising red flags in my mind, and prompting me to question their true intentions. Rumblings about the gang's ambitions to expand their control over Chicago only added to the complexity of the situation.

As I finally hit his pillow, I found myself consumed by the intricacies of the case. The pieces of the puzzle seemed increasingly elusive, leaving me with a sense of unease. Despite the looming uncertainty, I remained steadfast in my determination to untangle the web of deceit and uncover the true motives behind Sully's death. But for now, it was time to quiet my mind and seek much-needed rest.

The next morning, I found myself a bit disoriented as I hurried to reach FBI headquarters. It was the eve of Halloween, and as I stepped into the bustling building, I found myself surrounded by a colorful array of costumes. Liz, dressed as Wonder Woman, greeted me with a super-hero smile. It seemed I had overlooked the memo about dressing up, hastily threw on my jacket, and sunglasses, and grabbed the quirky alien weapon I put in my car, not wanting to feel left out.

"Hey, Rico! How was the party last night? Any new leads on Sully's case?" Liz inquired.

I adjusted my sunglasses with a sigh. "Not much to report. Everything seemed quiet. I was hoping you'd have some fresh intel by now."

Liz shook her head. "Nope, nothing yet. The Bad Town Faction operates with ironclad secrecy. Anyone who talks ends up in trouble. It's like they have a code: 'You talk, you're toast!'"

Lieutenant Guild sauntered into the room, decked out as Colonel Wilhelm Klink from Hogan's Heroes. Rico recognized the character immediately, though it seemed lost on most of the younger agents. To them, it was merely a matter of political correctness, questioning the appropriateness of dressing as a Nazi soldier. Guild's struggle to keep his monocle in place added a touch of authenticity to his portrayal, reminiscent of the iconic image that birthed countless monocle-wearing villains of the 20th century.

Surrounded by the murmurs of discomfort and raised eyebrows at Guild's costume choice, I remained focused on the task at hand. As the agents filed into the briefing room, the air was thick with the scent of stale coffee and lingering tension. The room was bathed in neon light, though a couple of long neon tubes flickered intermittently, casting long shadows across the walls. The walls themselves were covered with pinboards, adorned with strings of evidence that resembled a chaotic spider's web.

The seating was sparse, with only enough chairs for two-thirds of the attendees, leaving five agents to stand awkwardly along the periphery. The eclectic mix of costumes worn by some agents added an air of surrealism to the otherwise serious setting, with Lieutenant Herman X. Guild—his full name getting stink-eye looks—standing out like a sore thumb in his Colonel Klink getup.

Yet, despite the bizarre tableau, a distinct hush fell over the room as Herman "Xzavier" Guild began to speak, commanding the attention of all present with the authority of a seasoned leader. It was a fittingly eccentric scene, with Guild's middle name prompting thoughts of winning a game of Scrabble with letters rarely used.

The pinboard, adorned with its helter-skelter entanglement, stood as a testament to the tangled complexity of the investigation. Depending on who you asked, it resembled an evidence board, a conspiracy theory chart, a crazy wall, or a murder map. At its apex was a photo of Sully, surrounded by snapshots of individuals from the Barbarotti Family and young black men from the Bad Town Faction.

Colonel Klink, aka Lieutenant Guild, approached the board and began naming the individuals depicted in the photos. I recognized Vinny and Ronnie, my disdain for the latter discernible. However, the faces of the Bad Town Faction members were unfamiliar to me. Jimmy Ef, Drake Stir, and Leroy—the man who had shot Sully and subsequently found himself on the receiving end of a bullet—were all new names on my radar.

Leroy's current location was a piece of vital information. He lay in the ICU at Advocate Trinity Hospital, one of Illinois' five Level I Trauma Centers, located on the South Side—a hotbed of activity for both crime and medical emergencies alike.

Lieutenant Guild's voice cut through the tension in the room, his words carrying the weight of urgency. "Today, we learned that Leroy Johnson, aka 'The Bull,' has been moved from the ICU to a secured room with two CPD guards. Still no word on the Bad Town Faction's next move. Our trusted informant, the one with insights into their plans, was found dead last night—a bullet to the head in a back alley. Now, others are hesitant to come forward, fearing the same fate. Snitches don't last long in their world."

He pressed on, his voice carrying the weight of urgency and authority. "Our primary lead now rests with Leroy. Agents Baas and Doucet, you're on the ground. Sorry, Liz, you'll have to ditch the costume for now. Head to Advocate Trinity Hospital and extract whatever information you can from him. Agents Muller and Deming, dive into the digital realm. Scour the 'Socials' for any traces of Leroy's activity, especially on the dark web. Agent Tailor and Agent Tait, another shooting demands our attention on the South Side. Investigate thoroughly and ascertain any potential ties to the BTF gang. The rest of you on this task force, it's time to think outside the box and unearth the hidden truths within."

The room fell silent, the gravity of the situation sinking in. Guild's gaze swept over the assembled agents. "We're flying blind here, people. But we know one thing: the Bad Town Faction will be at Sully Barbarotti's funeral. That's our next point of interest. Listen to the streets and gather intel. Someone out there knows something, and we need to find them."

As Guild concluded, his words hung in the air like a call to arms. "Happy Halloween, everyone. But remember, the real danger isn't the ghosts and goblins—it's the gangs and the disorder they bring. Let's get to work."

As Liz and I drove to Advocate Trinity Hospital, I decided to take my car, eager to maintain some semblance of control during the frenzy of the investigation. I announced to Liz I was going to call Tito.

Liz couldn't help but tease me, "Seriously, Rico, are you two already married? Tito can handle a morning without you checking in every five minutes."

I felt a surge of irritation at the comment, my jaw tightening slightly. "I'm not checking in; I'm staying informed. This case is unpredictable, and I need to know if anything has changed since I left last night."

Realizing she may have struck a nerve, Liz quickly backpedaled. "Hey, just friendly banter, Rico. Didn't mean to push a button."

I sighed, feeling the tension drain from my shoulders as I took a deep breath. I dialed Tito's number, hoping for an update on how the party ended, but most importantly, to see if anything out of the ordinary had occurred.

"Hey, Tito, good morning," I greeted him, my voice laced with concern. As Tito's mumbled response reached my ears, I nodded, absorbing the information. "Late night, huh? Take it easy and catch some more sleep. Liz and I are grabbing an early lunch, so if I don't pick up, we're probably chowing down."

A brief pause ensued before I chuckled. "By the way, your dad's seemed cool about us. Glad he's on board. Hey, any plans for dinner tonight? How about an early dinner and movie afterwards? Who knows, maybe we'll make our own movie at my place later! Ha ha! See you at 5:30. Say hi to your folks for me."

"Well, that was utterly disgusting and made me want to throw up a little," Liz remarked, her comment landing like a punch and leaving Rico momentarily stunned. "Do you guys always talk that way? Gay men are so different than gay women."

I bristled at the implication, a flash of frustration crossing my features. "What should we be talking about, HGTV instead, and how to build a house?" I retorted; my tone tinged with sarcasm. "Let's not start stereotyping each other. It's enough when straights do it to us!"

Liz's apology felt like a small reprieve, her words softening the tension that had settled between us. "Sorry, it's just not what I'm used to in Lesbian circles," Liz admitted, her tone carrying a hint of discomfort.

Before any further damage could be done to our rapport, we arrived at the hospital and shifted gears to strategize our approach. I took the lead, recognizing that Leroy wouldn't be forthcoming with information voluntarily. "We'll need to catch him off guard somehow. You want to start, or should I?"

Liz answered, "Let's just play it by ear."

After navigating the labyrinthine corridors of the hospital, we finally reached Leroy's room, where one of the two CPD officers stood watch. Introducing ourselves and flashing our FBI badges, we inquired about any updates.

Officer Cunnings, a burly figure with a no-nonsense demeanor and a closely cropped salt-and-pepper beard, greeted us with a skeptical look in his steely eyes. "Good luck to you both," he grumbled, his voice carrying the weight of countless late-night patrols. "The only thing he's said to us is 'Fuck you!'"

As he spoke, the other officer, a younger man with a weary expression and a mop of unruly brown hair, returned from a quick trip to the vending machine, holding a steaming cup of coffee.

As we entered the room, the unmistakable scent of a hospital filled our nostrils—a sterile blend of gauze and antiseptic, punctuated by the rhythmic beeping of monitoring devices. Leroy's eyes flickered as we approached, but he remained silent.

I stepped forward, my voice steady. "Leroy Johnson, I'm Agent Rico Baas, and this is Agent Liz Doucet. We're with the FBI and would like to ask you a couple of questions."

Leroy's response was swift and sharp. "Fuck off!"

Leroy Johnson, lying in a prone position on the hospital bed, exuded a sense of hardened resilience. His muscular frame, adorned with a myriad of tattoos depicting gang symbols and cryptic imagery, hinted at a life entrenched in street culture. A gold teeth grill glinted in the dim light of the hospital room, a testament to his status as a high-ranking member of the underworld.

Despite his tough exterior, his face bore the scars of countless battles, a roadmap of the violence that permeated his world. As he glared at us with intense, unwavering eyes, it was clear that Leroy Johnson was not one to be trifled with.

I pressed on, fabricating a narrative about Sully's demise, hoping to elicit a reaction. "Well, Leroy, we understand you, Jimmy Ef and Drake Stir were involved in some sort of side hustle with the guns. That's what they've already confessed to. Sully had paid you for two hundred, but you decided to kill him for the rest of the money you hustled, even though you knew there would be consequences?"

Leroy's chest rose and fell rapidly, his anger unmistakable. "Fuck your consequences and fucking theories! You're full of shit!"

My brow furrowed as I met Leroy's glare head-on. "Now I know why they call you the bull—because you're full of it!"

Leroy's heartbeat quickened, his breaths shallow. "You fucking have no clue! He spat, his words dripping with venomous disdain. "I thought Sully was Sal 'cause I never seen him up close before, only from a distance." His voice crackled with raw hostility; each syllable laced with the deep-seated animosity he harbored towards those who represented everything he despised.

Liz, observing the tension, interjected with a firm tone. "And you knew what Salvador Barbarotti looked like, Because?" Her words faltered slightly as she glanced at Leroy's gold-grilled teeth, a discomfort crossing his features. It was as though she found herself addressing a character from a freakish circus sideshow, the incongruity of the situation adding an unsettling layer to her inquiry.

Leroy scoffed, his voice dripping with disdain. "All white guys with a beard look the same to me," he sneered, his words laced with a simmering hatred. His eyes bore into Liz with a cold intensity, his gaze filled with contempt and mistrust. The tension in the room thickened each word from Leroy's lips, adding another layer of hostility to the atmosphere.

Liz's eyes narrowed slightly, her expression stern. "Well, isn't that just a fascinating perspective," she remarked dryly, her tone thick with sarcasm. "All white guys look the same, huh? So, does every black guy look alike, too?"

Leroy's rage surged; his words were laced with accusations. "You clueless pigs ain't got a damn clue! You think you can waltz in here and play detective, but you ain't worth shit. You'll never understand what we gotta do to survive. You think you're tough? You're nothing but a couple of punks playing dress-up and you ain't got the balls to handle living in my hood. So don't come in here acting like you know shit about me or my life."

"Excuse me," I retorted, my voice unwavering, "We haven't we been anything but polite to you?" The intensity in my gaze matched Leroy's fury. "You've got some issues to deal with, but we just want to know why you shot Sully when you wanted to shoot Salvador Barbarotti."

Leroy's tone hardened, his words dripping with defiance. "I shot Sully 'cause I thought it was Sal, and there's a hit on Salvador Barbarotti," his confession edged with a hint of menace.

Liz leaned forward, her expression intense. "A hit? What do you mean a contract?"

Leroy's demeanor shifted, his tone growing defensive. "The person who offs Greasy Hands Salv scores twenty grand! Screw the two hundred guns—I'm just after the easy money!"

Sensing an opening, I pressed for more details. "Money from who?"

Leroy's reply came quick and sharp. "The Gangster Collection—easy money! Like I said."

My expression remained impassive as I delivered the final blow, My words once more laced with biting sarcasm. "Guess it wasn't that easy, huh? Here you are, lying with a bullet in your gut and nothing to show for it. Sounds like you could use a lawyer. Best of luck with that." My expression remained stoic as I concluded, my words dripping with disdain. "Well, Leroy, it's been a pleasure. You have a great morning."

Leroy's parting words were venomous, his tone oozing with contempt. "Fuck you!"

As Liz and I exited Leroy's room, we were met with the bewildered expressions of the two CPD officers stationed outside. Liz extended her hand for a congratulatory high-five, impressed by my deftness in extracting information from Leroy. Yet, beneath the surface, it was more than a mere celebration between colleagues; it was a subtle declaration to the CPD that the FBI was one step closer to cracking the case wide open.

I, however, downplayed my accomplishment, attributing it to teamwork. I probed into a discussion about the evolving nature of modern gangs, emphasizing the imperative for law enforcement not only to prosecute but also to deter gang activity through comprehensive societal interventions. I spoke passionately about the allure of gangs, acknowledging their appeal in providing social bonds and a sense of identity, yet lamenting the destructive path they paved. My words carried a weight of determination, a fervent desire to break the cycle of violence and despair that ensnared countless young lives.

As we made our way back to headquarters, Liz and I discussed our strategy for documenting Leroy's confession. Liz characterized my approach as, "effectively getting under Leroy's skin and pushing all his buttons."

However, my primary concern was the gravity of our discovery: a contract out on Salvador Barbarotti, worth a hefty $20K, with potential threats extending to other family members, including Tito. Red alarm bells rang in my mind as I contemplated how to discreetly warn Tito without revealing my true occupation.

Liz leaned in, sensing what was on my mind, her voice low and urgent, as she sought to impress upon me the gravity of the situation. "You could single-handedly ignite a gang war if you let slip to Tito, who will undoubtedly inform his father. Think this through," she warned me.

Liz continued, "We need to tread carefully here. Our priority is to compile our report and ensure that Lieutenant Guild ramps up surveillance now that we have a clearer understanding of what we're up against. You must remain close to Tito; the danger is imminent, and they could strike at any moment. With the funeral just around the corner, we cannot afford any missteps. We must navigate through this period unscathed before divulging anything to the Barbarotti Family."

Upon our return to headquarters, the room hummed with activity. Colleagues exchanged hurried words and the click of keyboards filled the air as agents diligently worked at their desks. A ripple of applause greeted Liz and my entrance, acknowledging our successful interrogation of Leroy "The Bull."

Emerging from his office, Lt. Guild, still dressed as Colonel Klink but missing his monocle, offered his commendation. "Nice work, agents!" he praised.

Liz, diverting the spotlight, gestured toward me. "Agent Baas has quite the knack for getting under people's skin," she noted with a wry smile.

I grinned in response. "No personal dig intended, Liz, right."

Turning to Lt. Guild, Rico sought an update on any developments. The lieutenant's response was both unexpected and significant: "Agent Deming discovered chatter on the dark web confirming a hit on the Barbarotti Family. While specifics about the money remain elusive, we now have verification from multiple sources. Both Sal Senior and Sal Junior are potential targets."

I was perplexed as to where the money came from for the hit contract. "The Gangster Collection put out the hit, but who paid for the hit?"

I voiced my concern to Lt. Guild, but he wasn't as concerned at this point and felt the primary goal was to either stop the hit contract or stop the Bad Town Faction who was already under investigation for gun running.

I proposed the idea of maintaining close proximity to Tito until we could resolve the threat against the family. "I believe it's crucial to establish a stronger connection with the Barbarotti Family and gather any pertinent information they might possess."

Lt. Guild cautioned, "Under no circumstances are you to disclose details about the contract hit."

I acknowledged the directive with a hint of frustration, "Of course, Lieutenant, I understand. However, I'll be armed at all times when around them."

"Excellent," replied Lt. Guild, emphasizing, "Stay in constant communication with Liz to avoid arousing suspicion. Also, consider having her accompany you to the funeral for added security."

Lt. Guild added, "We'll have ground personnel and a sharpshooter on standby if necessary. Do you have the location for the funeral yet?"

I recalled a conversation at the Halloween party between Sal, Tito's father, and Maxine, Sully's widow, about potential locations.

"I overheard talk of St. Vincent de Paul, but Sully and Maxine attended St. Mary of the Angels. I'll confirm the details," I assured Lt. Guild, clarifying his commitment to obtaining the necessary information.

CHAPTER 8

Rico

The day's drama and the daunting task of documenting every detail devoured more time than I could have imagined. As the clock mercilessly struck four P.M., I felt the weight of my impending date at 5:30, a rumble of hunger reminding me of the lunch I never had.

Craving cleanliness after rubbing elbows with the underworld, I plotted a pit stop for some fast food and a quick douche to shake off the grime. The mere thought of arriving fresh and clean for Tito spurred me on, meticulously timing each move to ensure I'd grace Tito's Brownstone with ten minutes to spare.

In perfect synchronization with my mental timetable, I arrived, dedicating a meticulous five minutes to sanitizing my phone, eradicating any lingering traces of communication from headquarters.

Concealment gnawed at me, a necessary evil in safeguarding my burgeoning relationship and newfound family, shielded from the perils of their shared underworld. My heart ached for simplicity, yearning to escape the looming specter of organized crime and its entanglements. Yet, duty tethered me to this turbulent world, my devotion to Tito compelling me forward despite the risks. With resolve, I hastened down the bustling street, navigating the maze of parked cars that punctuated the Wrigley Park area, minor inconveniences paling compared to the allure of Tito's chosen haven in the heart of the city.

* * * *

Tito

With my radiant smile, I greeted Rico at the door, and in an instant, we were enveloped in each other's arms, the world melting away in the warmth of our embrace. With a surge of passion, Rico lifted me off my feet, our lips meeting in a fervent kiss that spoke volumes of his longing.

I was awestruck by Rico's ardor and marveled at the intensity of our reunion, savoring the sweet yearning that had built in our brief separation.

"Being apart certainly has its perks," I quipped, my eyes twinkling with affection. "But nothing compares to being in your arms again."

Rico's response was immediate, his voice laced with sincerity. "I could spend eternity with you and still crave every moment like it's the first time."

Our kiss deepened, a testament to our unyielding desire, as Rico guided me into my bedroom, shutting out the world with a gentle click of the door. With practiced finesse, Rico's hands moved to unbutton my pants, and though I slightly objected to the intimacy to come, I found myself surrendering to him as he pressed me against the door, my protests mere whispers against the symphony of our passion.

As Rico got onto his knees, he started working me over good without a fight... my objections turned into pleas to keep going... ending with a stifled moan of pleasure that rendered my body limp.

Rico didn't factor this episode into his tightly packed schedule and realized we had to be on our way to eat dinner and catch a movie lickity-split. (Okay, yes, pun intended)

We hustled our way to Portillo's Restaurants, an iconic spot known for its fast-casual service and quintessential Chicago-style cuisine, such as hot dogs, Maxwell Street Polish, and Italian beef. It was Rico's first time experiencing this must-visit Chicago dining gem.

Rico remarked, "I feel like I'm stepping back in time to the nostalgic era of the 1960s, surrounded by vintage memorabilia and retro charm."

As we entered, Rico continued to marvel at the ambiance, exclaiming, "It's like being transported to a bygone era, a classic American diner straight out of a movie!"

We quickly perused the menu and placed our orders, eagerly anticipating our meal as we discussed which movie to see. With no tickets purchased yet, we remained undecided about the prospect of a midweek outing. We both settled on "Oppenheimer," a sprawling biographical drama featuring Cillian Murphy as J. Robert Oppenheimer, the enigmatic physicist behind the development of the atomic bomb during the Manhattan Project. It promised to be a cinematic journey worth embarking on, and we looked forward to sharing the experience, relishing the simple joy of our first movie theater outing in each other's company.

The evening unfolded like a dream, with laughter filling the air as we savored our meal, immersed ourselves in the captivating narrative of "Oppenheimer," and relished each other's company. As the credits rolled, Rico extended an invitation for me to spend the night, to which I hesitantly agreed, suggesting, "You know, you could just stay here tonight."

Rico countered with a mischievous grin, "But I have something special waiting for you at my place, and besides, I feel like it's my turn to host after our little marathon of visits to your place and your parent's house. Let's head to my place tonight."

"All right, you win," I conceded, flashing a sly smile. "But first, let's swing by my house so I can park my car, then we can cruise over to your place to prevent me from looking for parking. After all, you have that sweet indoor parking spot in your building, right?"

Rico chuckled, "You got it, boss. I'm here to please!" With a playful exchange of keys and a quick shuffle of automobiles, I hopped into Rico's stylish Ford Mach-E, also an electric marvel. Rico, however, felt more like he was driving a sleek sports car instead of a Tesla, which he jokingly dubbed "the Leer Jet."

Once we arrived at Rico's place and ascended the elevator to the ninetieth floor, we paused to admire the sparkling city lights below. Rico then brought out a special wine from California, a wine he had procured directly from Sebastiani in Sonoma Valley. It was one of their award-winning selections from the Reserve Collection, a fine Cabernet Sauvignon.

Rico regaled me with the story of how he acquired the wine during a memorable wine-tasting excursion with a close friend and a woman named Mary, who had retired in the Sonoma area.

Knowing my appreciation for fine wines, Rico's gesture was met with surprise and delight. As Rico let the wine breathe, we both engaged in a lively conversation about the wineries in Northern California. I revealed that I had explored various regions, "I've been all around the Northern California vineyards including Napa Valley and lesser-known vineyards tucked behind the hills of Oakland. But I prefer the top wineries in Oakland and the East Bay over Napa Valley." I admitted that I hadn't yet visited the wineries in Sonoma.

We reveled in the complex flavors and the lingering oakiness of the Sebastiani Cabernet, each sip igniting a fire within them. Rico couldn't resist sharing the tantalizing details about the oak barrels, boasting that they were the oldest in California, imparting a unique and unforgettable taste to the wine.

As the night grew late, Rico had more surprises in store for me, leading me to the bedroom with a naughty glint in his eye. Our bodies moved together in a passionate dance, fueled by desire and longing. The romantic foreplay escalated, each touch sending shivers down my spine as I surrendered to the intoxicating allure of his love.

In the throes of passion, I realized that I had fallen deeply for Rico, my heart overflowing with emotions, but I dared not voice them just yet. I couldn't shake the feeling that Rico might feel the same way, our connection noticeable in every touch and whispered promise.

We ended up falling asleep in each other's arms, wrapped in the warmth of our shared love until a sudden jolt disrupted our peaceful slumber. My eyes shot open, as my heart pounded in my chest to an urgent alarm blared from my phone.

"What was that?" Rico's voice cut through the darkness, filled with concern.

"It's an emergency alert," I replied, my voice tinged with apprehension. "I set it up for my family to contact me in case of emergencies." With trembling hands, I reached for my phone, my heart racing with a sense of dread. Dialing my mom's number, I felt a racing pulse as fearful possibilities raced through my mind with each passing moment.

My mother's voice, laden with sorrow and urgency, cut through the line, delivering shattering news. "Thank God you're alive, son," her words heavy with emotion. "But brace yourself, Tito. Your place is on fire. Someone threw a pipe bomb, and it exploded. Your dad's surveillance cameras and alarms alerted us immediately. The fire department is already there, but I'm sorry, son, everything is gone. Your house, your clothes, all your belongings except for your car. It was parked behind the house and was damaged by the blast, but it's still drivable."

The news of the bombing shattered the peace of our intimate refuge, leaving us both reeling in its wake. Rico watched helplessly as my composure crumbled, my knees buckling under the weight of the devastating revelation. The inferno consuming my home seemed to mirror the inferno raging within our souls, fueled by fear and uncertainty as my expression shifted from confusion to despair.

Clutching my hand tightly, Rico vowed, "I'll stand by your side through the darkest hours, our love will serve as a beacon of hope in the face of adversity."

As we began to confront the grim details, Rico's mind raced with ominous possibilities. The Bad Town Faction Gang had finally made their move, and now we were confronted with the chilling reality that nowhere was safe. The flames licking at my home served as a stark reminder of the danger lurking in the shadows, ready to consume us at any moment.

With each passing second, the urgency of our situation intensified. Rico felt a surge of protectiveness wash over him, a fierce determination to shield me from the storm raging outside. But as we hurried to leave Rico's apartment, a sense of foreboding settled over us like a suffocating blanket. The night was far from over, and the darkness held more secrets than we dared to imagine.

Once Rico and I arrived, we were met with a devastating sight—nothing remained but ashes, the remnants of my cherished memories. The acrid scent of smoke lingered in the air, assaulting our senses, and evoking a profound sense of loss. My eyes, red-rimmed from the lingering smoke and ash, scanned the desolate landscape, each charred beam and crumbling wall a painful reminder of what once was.

"All my memories are gone," I lamented, my voice heavy with sorrow.

Rico wrapped his arms around me, the warmth of his embrace a beacon of comfort amidst my desolation. "They're just material things, Tito," Rico murmured softly, his words a gentle reminder of life's enduring treasures. "You're alive, and your memories remain intact. Everything else can be replaced," he reassured, his voice filled with compassion.

I buried my head into Rico's chest, overcome with emotion. "It could have been both of us. I'm so sorry for putting you in harm's way," I confessed between sobs. Rico held me tighter, his heart aching for my pain.

"It's not your fault, Tito. But it's a stark reminder to steer clear of organized crime. You're a natural leader, and you can achieve greatness in any endeavor," Rico affirmed, his words laced with conviction.

Just then, Virginia and Sal, my parents, approached us, concern etched on their faces. "Are you both okay?" Virginia inquired—her voice filled with worry. I nodded, my gratitude toward Rico evident. "If it weren't for Rico, we would both have been inside," I admitted, my voice trembling with emotion.

Rico chimed in, emphasizing the gravity of the situation. "It was merely luck; this is unbelievable. Who can prepare for something like this?"

Nothing could have fully prepared us for the harrowing turn of events. It was unquestionably a stroke of luck, perhaps guided by a subconscious intuition or even divine intervention, that the two of us ended up in Rico's apartment. In hindsight, the decision proved crucial, saving both our lives.

As the gravity of the situation sank in, Rico recognized the imminent danger they had narrowly escaped. The thought of further assassination attempts loomed ominously, prompting Rico to cling to me even tighter, determined to keep me safe at all costs.

Virginia and Sal joined us, and we formed a group hug. Sal spoke with determination, "With each passing moment, the urgency of our situation becomes increasingly apparent, fueling our resolve to safeguard ourselves from further threats."

"Someone wants to erase the Barbarotti Family leadership, but they won't succeed," Sal continued, his voice echoing with steely resolve amid the desolation of my charred home. "This isn't merely an attack on property; it's a direct assault on our legacy, our heritage," he emphasized, his tone grave yet unwavering. "But mark my words, whoever dares to challenge us will face not only the strength of our resolve but also the full force of our family's unyielding spirit. They may have scorched your home, Tito, but they will never extinguish the flame of our legacy."

CHAPTER 9

Tito

My dad, Greasy Hands Salv, mindful of the recent attack on my home and wary of drawing any more unwanted attention, opted to hold an emergency family meeting, but not at our home. It was a decision born out of necessity and a healthy dose of paranoia—after all, who wants a side of pipe bomb with their pepperoni?

Under my counsel, we settled on a last-minute change of venue: Jimmy's Pizza, the bustling family-owned joint out in the burbs.

"Better to be safe and stuffed with cheesy goodness," Rico quipped, trying to lighten the mood as we made our way to Fox Lake near the Wisconsin border. I nodded in agreement, appreciating Rico's knack for finding humor in even dire predicaments.

As we arrived at Jimmy's Pizza, the sight of our extended family gathered around pool tables and arcade games provided a surreal contrast to the gravity of the situation.

"Looks like the only thing missing is Uncle Vito trying to hustle everyone at foosball," Rico quipped again, earning a chuckle from me.

Drowning in the absurdity of it all, the Barbarotti Clan scrambled to find a seat among the flurry of greetings that seemed to spiral out of control. Rico and I sought a brief respite to listen to the proceedings. I, in particular, dreaded any further condolences regarding the destruction of my home, each remark feeling like salt rubbed into my wounds.

However, as the weight of the situation converged on the family, my uncles and cousins offered their condolences in their customary manner—embraces and kisses exchanged between men, a tradition I found oddly comforting. Despite my initial desire to distance myself from further reminders of loss, I gradually realized the significance of this tradition to everyone in the family and found solace in accepting their compassion.

* * * *

Rico

With each heartfelt embrace Tito received, I discreetly gauged the mood, keenly aware of the potential for heightened emotions and impulsive reactions.

Navigating the solemn occasion, my thoughts drifted to Liz, my liaison between me and FBI headquarters. I knew she would be orchestrating behind the scenes, leveraging the bureau's resources to investigate the bombing. Given the seriousness of the matter, I understood the urgency of their efforts.

Amid the family's grief, my phone buzzed with a message from Liz. Her update confirmed his suspicions—Lt. Guild and the FBI were already on the case, utilizing street cameras near Wrigley Stadium to identify the perpetrators. I felt a glimmer of hope knowing that law enforcement was mobilizing to prevent further violence.

LT. Guild felt confident they would put out an APB—All Points Bulletin on what they were not only calling an arsonist but also labeling as domestic terrorism to prompt Homeland Security's involvement. This way, special funds through the Domestic Terrorism Prevention Act for the Department of Homeland Security and the FBI to combat far-right violence would be utilized. Even though the FBI suspected this was a Bad Town Faction gang attack, labeling them a far-right group as well might be a way of shutting them down completely.

Liz let me know that they were going to court to get the warrants and authority necessary to protect Americans from terrorism. I thanked Liz for the update and hoped that this would end the group before a full-on gang war erupted. But was the planning of a gang war already in the works?

* * * *

Tito

I observed my dad address the Family, silently taking in his measured yet resolute words. A man of action, Greasy Hands Salv wasn't one to shy away from getting his hands dirty when the situation demanded it. The room reeked with tension; the collective anger of the family was certain as they shifted restlessly in their seats. I could see the fire burning deeply within them, the hunger for revenge consuming their every thought.

However, Sal remained composed, his words cutting through the thick hostility like a knife. He understood the importance of strategic retaliation, not blind passion, in confronting their adversaries.

Addressing our gathered family members, Sal's voice pierced through the charged atmosphere with clarity and purpose.

"We've been targeted by the BTF on multiple occasions now, it has become plainly clear, first with Sully's death, and now with the attempted murder of my son and his friend Rico by blowing up Tito's home. It was a senseless and unprovoked attack, and it's clear the BTF aims to seize control of our territory. But we won't concede it," he declared firmly, adding, "They didn't want to come to the funeral to give their condolences; they wanted to catch us all together to kill as many of us as possible."

The room erupted in a chorus of cheers and calls for vengeance, but Sal raised a hand to quell the fervor, pressing on with his address.

"The BTF is engaged in a bloody gang war of their own on the South Side, resorting to drive-by shootings and pipe-bomb attacks. This isn't just organized crime—it's terrorism, plain and simple. Engaging them directly would lead to dire consequences, as they have no regard for human life, be it women, children, or their own members."

Salvatore then outlined a strategic approach, leveraging the alliances the family already had with the Gangster Collection, one of Chicago's largest street gangs.

"Instead of plunging headlong into a war, let's work with our allies to dismantle the BTF," he proposed. "The Gangster Collection, led by Luther Hoops, who's been running the operation from behind bars since his life sentence last year, is well aware of the importance of community respect and legitimacy. They share our goal of improving our communities' reputations and can be valuable partners in this endeavor."

As Salvatore laid out his plan, the family members listened attentively, initially unsure of his direction but gradually warming to the logic behind his words. Then, with a simple yet strategic proposition, Sal outlined a path forward that minimized confrontation while maximizing the potential for success. "If the BTF has put a price on my head and my son's head, then we'll make it clear to the Gangster Collection that we're willing to pay for each BTF board member they eliminate," he concluded. "This way, we can achieve our goals without getting our hands dirty and avoid drawing unwanted attention from law enforcement."

* * * *

Rico

In the subsequent silence, I found myself admiring Salvatore's strategic finesse, acknowledging the perceptiveness in his handling of the intensifying situation. However, the prospect of orchestrating hits carried its inherent legal repercussions, potentially resulting in life sentences.

Yet, I hoped a solution could be negotiated with the FBI—a win-win scenario, offering the Gangster Collection's incarcerated leader, Luther Hoops, a route to mitigate the conflict. Instead of resorting to lethal force, they could set a trap, ensuring the apprehension and incarceration of all involved, effectively quelling the Bad Town Faction while sparing unnecessary bloodshed.

The meeting concluded with Sal's booming voice reverberating through the room, demanding a decisive response: "What say you? Yes, or no?" In response, a cacophony of affirmative chants echoed from the majority of attendees, resounding with emotional "Yes, yes, yes" declarations. However, I noticed a dissenting voice—Ronnie Barbarotti's emphatic "Hell No, Hell No!" While unanimity remained elusive, there existed a noticeable consensus toward pursuing the least sordid path to resolve the crisis.

With the decision at hand, Sal took the floor to announce the location for Sully's funeral. Typically, funerals would be held in the parish church of the deceased, yet Sully's connection to St. Vincent De Paul Catholic Church presented a unique opportunity. "Many of us, including Sully's wife and children, regularly attend St. Vincent's, and the church has graciously agreed to host the Funeral Mass. The

Funeral Director will collaborate with the priests to prepare for the service, which will take place on November 8 at three P.M."

Sal continued, "There is one important detail to note: due to unforeseen circumstances, Sully was already cremated. While some may wonder about the compatibility of cremation with Catholic funeral rites, the Church maintains that cremation does not preclude one from receiving a funeral liturgy. However, until we have the BTF situation under control, heightened vigilance is imperative, and access will be restricted to family members only."

* * * *

Tito

Rico remained steadfast by my side as my father delivered his address, and once my dad had concluded, Rico turned to me.

"Can I come to the Funeral Mass, Tito?" he asked. "I thought I might attend with Liz. She's been a rock lately, and she really wants to help us through this."

I nodded, my expression grateful. "Of course, you're coming with me. And I don't think my dad will have any issue with Liz either but let me ask him to make sure."

Curious about my thoughts post-speech, Rico sought my perspective. "What did you make of your dad's words?"

Still grappling with the shock of losing everything I owned, I took a moment to collect my thoughts.

"I think whatever we can do to end this derangement with killings and bombings needs to be done. But I'm not sold on cozying up to another gang. I don't trust them. These black gangs have no regard for life, and drive-by shootings are almost a daily occurrence on the South Side now. Can you imagine if that starts happening all around us here, too? No, this madness needs to stop."

Rico empathized with my plight and offered his support. "Tito, stay with me for now until things settle," he suggested. "I've spoken to Liz, and she said you could use her room for personal space if you'd like. She's caught up in homemaking with her girlfriend, and I barely see her except at work."

I embraced Rico warmly. "I'd love to stay with you and share your bed. If I could use the other room for my belongings…I still have some stuff at my parent's house, but maybe we can go shopping later to replace certain necessities that were lost."

As my emotions surged once more, Rico squeezed my hand reassuringly. "We'll weather this storm together, Tito. I promise. Things will get better, and we'll emerge stronger for it. Trust me."

Salvador Barbarotti stood outside the Pizza Parlor; his gaze fixed on me approaching. As I neared, my father enveloped me in a tight embrace, his grip conveying both strength and concern.

"How are you holding up, son?" My Dad's voice carried a weight of empathy, tinged with a hint of steel. "Devastated about your place I'm sure, but don't worry, we'll find you something else. Still bunking with Rico?"

My response carried a hint of uncertainty, my words tinged with unspoken apprehension.

"Yeah, that's what I wanted to discuss with you. Rico's been my anchor since the bombing. He's offered me a place to stay until things settle down. Feels safer up there, high above the madness in that fortress of a high-rise apartment."

Sal nodded, his expression a blend of empathy and determination. "Rico's practically family now, Tito. He's expected at Sully's funeral."

I concurred, "Rico's roommate Liz wants to come, too. She's been a pillar of support for both of us, and she's even offered up her room for my belongings."

Sal responded, "Of course, Liz is also welcome to join us."

Sal's eyes hardened with resolve. "I promise you, son, I'll handle this. When you take over, there won't be a trace of the BTF's havoc. They'll feel the full force of our retaliation."

My reply was measured, tinged with caution. "I'd rather see them rot in a cell. We can't risk you getting entangled in legal troubles and end in jail." My worry hung heavily in the air, the recent turmoil casting a shadow over our world.

Sal's reassurance was unwavering. "After the funeral, we'll strategize. Your input is invaluable, son. Oh, and about your firearm…was it lost in the fire?"

I paused, lost in thought. "Yeah, last I remember, it was in my safe."

Sal persisted, seeking to reassure me. "I'll get you a new piece right away," he asserted, his tone carrying the authority of his position. "Keep it close until this storm passes. Understood?"

I nodded solemnly, the burden of responsibility settling heavily on my shoulders.

I strolled back to Rico, a grin lighting up my face. "Let's head back to your place and do something to distract me from all this lunacy." Rico chuckled, nodding. "Right, our place it is (with emphasis on 'our'). Looks like we're officially roomies now, whether we planned it or not!"

I flashed a mischievous smile. "Home, James, and make it snappy! I need my Calgon moment."

Rico laughed, then asked, "Anything else I can do to lift your spirits?"

I raised an eyebrow playfully. "Hmm, let me think about that. I'm sure I can come up with a few ideas." Rico grinned back, replying, "I'm sure I can help with getting it up—oops, I mean with the 'come up' part."

As we cruised homeward, I suggested we take a detour to the Fashion Outlets of Chicago off the 294 freeway. Rico, who hadn't yet ventured out for shopping since his arrival in Chicago, eagerly agreed. Spotting the unmistakable signs for the outlet mall, Rico took the exit, leading us to a shopper's paradise.

At the helm of our shopping adventure, my eyes gleamed at the sight of the Nike Factory Store right up front, and I declared it the perfect starting point. In just thirty minutes, I was already laden with new sports gear. Then, I suddenly remembered my predicament after the fire had left me underwear-less. So, the Calvin Klein store was next on my agenda.

Rico, in jest, remarked, "Well, I know someone who always gets between you and your Calvin's!"

His comment elicited a hearty burst of laughter from me, a delightful sound that lifted the weight of recent somberness, much to Rico's relief, I'm sure.

With over a hundred and fifty stores to explore, Rico relinquished control to me and my whims, content to follow my lead. My desire to purchase something for Rico prompted his playful suggestion of a late lunch at China Wok, eliciting a knowing grin from him. Encumbered with bags, we eagerly made our way to lunch, marveling at our successful spree in such a short time.

After lunch, it was time to return to the sanctuary of our sky-rise retreat. As I mulled over the logistics of getting our haul back to the apartment, I voiced my weariness and desire for a foot massage, which Rico readily assented to. The prospect of another bottle of wine, perhaps a Merlot with a captivating backstory, only added to our ardor.

Rico regaled me with the tale of how he stumbled upon this particular wine, a blend concocted by one of the brothers at Sebastiani's in Sonoma. Dubbed Smoking Loon, this blend was once a luxury reserved for elite patrons, commanding a price of sixty-four dollars per bottle. Yet, fortune smiled upon us as it became available to the masses through Albertsons on the West Coast or Jewel-Osco in Chicago, priced at a mere $16.50 per bottle. We made another quick stop as Rico couldn't wait to purchase a couple of bottles and get home to share it with me.

"Let's split up, take separate elevators up," Rico proposed as we reached the St. Regis. With a mountain of bags in tow, we finally reunited at our front door, greeted by a scene reminiscent of Christmas morning. "Looks like we've got some unpacking to do, but at least we can tackle it together," Rico remarked with a grin.

I couldn't help but return the smile, feeling a sense of relief wash over me. At that moment, I began to see my ordeal as more than just a setback—it was the prologue to a new chapter, an adventure waiting to unfold. And at the heart of it all was one undeniable truth: I had found someone special to share it with—Rico.

In the days that followed, Rico and I settled into our new routines, exploring the depths of our connection in every facet of our lives. Beyond sharing workouts, meals, and movies, they reveled in intimate moments together, cherishing the simple joys of mutual massages, shared showers, and passionate lovemaking. Despite our separate obligations, we always found time to be together, enveloped in the warmth of each other's presence.

As the weekend drew near, I eagerly anticipated uninterrupted time with my special someone, relishing the chance to deepen our bond even further. While I harbored deeper feelings of falling in love, I decided to wait until after the funeral to broach the topic, content with the monumental change of living together for now.

While we were chilling at home, Rico announced to me that he had to leave for a short while to attend a work meeting, so I decided to clean up the place and be domestic. I was already used to doing my own laundry, but I threw in Rico's as well. Might as well do both at the same time and save energy.

* * * *

Rico

I went to work to investigate who the person or persons were who blew up Tito's house. I had a meeting with Lt. Guild, Liz, and the others on the task force regarding catching those in the BTF who were involved. I got the whole task force up to speed regarding what the Barbarotti Family, led by Salvador, had planned.

I laid out my idea of having the FBI negotiate a win-win scenario by offering the Gangster Collection's incarcerated leader, Luther Hoops, a route to mitigate the conflict.

I gave them my pitch, "Instead of resorting to lethal force, we could set a trap, ensuring the apprehension and incarceration of all involved, effectively quelling the Bad Town Faction while sparing unnecessary bloodshed. I have written down my thoughts to show everyone, and I hope I can convince the task force to prevent as much bloodshed as possible."

I presented a good argument and my well-thought-through plan, seeking to persuade the task force. I believed failure to persuade them could escalate tensions into a full-scale conflict between the BTF and the Barbarotti Family, posing an existential threat to the safety of citizens in the greater Chicago area.

I persisted in my desire to converse with Luther Hoops, believing it crucial to explore all avenues of negotiation. However, the Lieutenant countered, asserting that existing contacts within the Gangster Collection, some of whom were involved in Luther's arrest, were better positioned to handle such delicate negotiations.

Yet, I argued, "Luther's influence, even from behind bars, could be instrumental in persuading the BTF to reconsider their actions. I propose a hypothetical scenario: Luther informing his cohorts of an imminent hit on the BTF board members, a move that could potentially deter their aggressive actions against the Barbarotti Family. Given Luther's history of racketeering and territorial disputes, the mere suggestion of his involvement could strike fear into the hearts of the BTF, potentially averting further violence."

Lieutenant Guild expressed his intention to deliberate further on my proposal and instructed the agents involved in Hoops' apprehension to be briefed on the potential utilization of his influence. Nevertheless, he emphasized that their immediate focus was on the upcoming funeral on Wednesday. Intelligence indicated a credible threat against Salvador Barbarotti during the procession, prompting coordination efforts with Homeland Security and SWAT teams to secure the vicinity and establish rapid-response measures.

Guild emphasized, "It is most important to maintain close proximity to Salvador and Tito," assigning me the role of their closest protector. To preempt any hostile actions from the BTF, additional measures were implemented, including the infiltration of undercover agents within the church congregation. Agents Deming and Muller would assume the guise of clergy members, tasked with ensuring the integrity of the church's interior while maintaining constant communication via discreet earpieces.

Acknowledging the weight of responsibility thrust upon me, I, still relatively new to the force, recognized the enormity of the task. While confident in my abilities, I harbored reservations, particularly concerning the potential for misinterpretation by others on the task force, as well as those in Homeland Security and the SWAT team. Vigilant and cautious, I vowed to preempt any escalation, prioritizing the protection of my beloved, Tito, above all else.

At present, my priority is to ensure a tranquil weekend with Tito, providing a respite before the impending week of heightened tension. It would be the first funeral I'd ever attended, and I didn't want it to be my last.

Before departing, I approached Lt. Guild with a request to wear soft armor, a bullet-proof concealable vest beneath my suit at the funeral. The Lieutenant commended my foresight, remarking, "That's a wise precaution. We'll arrange for vests for Liz and the other two agents as well. You're thinking ahead, Agent Baas, giving yourself the tactical advantage. Stay vigilant and assess every angle and possibility before taking your seat. With your background, you're adept at anticipating the mindset of a gang member."

Heading back home, I made a conscious effort to set aside thoughts of the funeral and my duties, wanting to savor the moments with Tito without distraction. I yearned to share every detail with him, but the timing was crucial; maintaining my cover was paramount until after the funeral.

So, for now, all I craved was to return home, plant a loving kiss on Tito's lips, unwind in front of the TV, and perhaps indulge in some pizza delivery. The comfort of living together suited me, and I cherished the routine of coming home to my man. I silently hoped that Tito felt the same ease and contentment in our shared space.

Despite the disarray we'd weathered in a short span, our connection felt natural, as if every piece of the puzzle fell effortlessly into place. I hesitated to overanalyze it, recognizing the blessing and curse of my mind's tendency to dissect every detail—a duality that shaped my perception of our budding relationship.

CHAPTER 10

Tito

Entering the dance with the unknown and navigating the ever-shifting landscape, I found solace in Rico's embrace. My burning desire to lead my mafia family into a new era clashed with external pressures from rival gangs. The world had evolved, marked by ubiquitous surveillance, advanced biometrics, and stringent government measures against organized crime. Despite this, I envisioned a transformation—a shift towards a streamlined, secure business model anchored in cryptocurrency and blockchain technology, safeguarding transactions from the ever-looming specter of cyber threats.

My family's ventures in the burgeoning CBD oil and medical marijuana industries hinted at vast financial gain, yet my true fulfillment lay in a realm untethered to the constraints of my criminal lineage. As I grappled with the weight of familial expectations and the allure of newfound possibilities, I pondered the question that lingered at the core of my being: What path would lead me to ultimate fulfillment and freedom, unencumbered by the shadows of the past?

Within me, I harbored a secret longing to share with Rico—a venture that would take us on a journey far from the familiar paths we tread. Even before Rico mused about visiting wineries in Sonoma, I had quietly explored the possibility of running my very own vineyard. Delving into my family history, I unearthed tales of my great-grandparents' expertise in grape cultivation and winemaking, our legacy echoing through the centuries from the sun-kissed shores of Sicily.

With its rich winemaking tradition shaped by ancient civilizations and a climate conducive to grape cultivation, Sicily held a special allure for me. I felt the call of winemaking coursing through my veins, a passion I had kept hidden until now. The destruction of my home only intensified this desire for change, prompting me to embrace the legacy of my ancestors in pursuit of a new beginning. More than anything, I desperately wanted to share my vision with Rico, to confide in him the dreams that had long simmered in the depths of my soul.

Sensing that Rico had other matters weighing heavily on his mind, I hesitated to broach the topic, recognizing that the timing might not be right. Nonetheless, I held onto the hope that soon I would be able to share my aspirations with him and embark on this new journey together. While I was eager to reveal my Epiphany to Rico, I understood the importance of approaching the subject with care. Perhaps a romantic evening with some great wine would be the perfect setting. For now, I'd hold onto this secret just a little longer.

* * * *

Rico

My thoughts swirled incessantly, fixating on the looming specter of Wednesday's funeral. I couldn't shake the feeling that whatever transpired would be profoundly life-altering. Offering a vague excuse to Tito about tending to work matters, I slipped out, drawn to Saint Vincent de Paul Catholic Church. Entering the hallowed space, I found myself enveloped in awe at the church's grandeur. The architecture seamlessly blended Romanesque and French Gothic elements, adorned with magnificent stained-glass windows and presided over by a majestic marble altar adorned with intricate carvings and mosaics.

As I marveled at the splendor, I also conducted a subtle reconnaissance, mapping out the layout of the church and noting potential hiding spots for any nefarious intruders. A priest approached, extending a warm welcome and inviting me to move closer, but I politely declined, preferring to soak in the scene from the back, quietly absorbing the solemnity and beauty of the surroundings.

To my astonishment, I spotted members of the Barbarotti Family seated in the church. Upon closer inspection, I discerned Salvador, Virginia, and Maxine with her two sons. Although I hadn't met Maxine's boys before, their resemblance to her description at the Halloween party left little doubt. Contemplating whether to approach them, I hesitated, wary of drawing attention to my presence. Instead, I quietly slipped away, reassured by the sight of the family and confident in the security measures in place for the funeral.

Exiting the church, I pondered over the proceedings, wondering whether there would be a procession to the burial grounds. However, I recalled that Sully had already been cremated, leading me to wonder about the protocol for a Funeral Mass honoring someone's ashes. As someone with a Lutheran upbringing, I found myself navigating unfamiliar customs and rituals, my church attendance limited to childhood memories and the occasional wedding ceremony of some college friends.

Returning to the apartment, I couldn't help but marvel at the deep-rooted devotion within the Barbarotti Family. Not that I lacked closeness with my own family back in California—my parents and sisters held a special place in my heart, with our bond unique in its own right, given the distance between us. I cherished my independence, a luxury I knew Tito didn't have, hoping we could find solace in each other's company.

I wondered how I could ever compete with a family that gathered for every birthday, boasting a legion of cousins on his father's side alone. While my familial circle was smaller, save for occasional visits to my grandparents in the Netherlands, I found comfort in their presence, alongside my friends. I knew I loved Tito, and despite the complexities of his family's ties to the mob, they were genuinely pleasant to be around. Contemplating the question of happiness, I wondered if I could find contentment in embracing Tito's expansive family. The scenario reminded me of the movie *My Big Fat Greek Wedding*, which, in my case, would be titled *My Big Fat Mob Family!*

* * * *

Tito

Upon returning to the apartment, Rico was greeted by a sight that sparked curiosity. I had returned from the market with an armful of groceries, prompting Rico to inquire, "What's the occasion? Are we expecting guests?"

With a playful twinkle in my eye, I responded, "Nope, just making you dinner for once. It's time you experienced the culinary prowess of the Barbarotti lineage. We all have the knack for cooking, but some husbands are just too lazy to bother."

Rico chuckled, "So, what's the occasion for this culinary showcase?"

I grinned and replied, "Consider it a token of my appreciation for everything you've done for me. And there's more to come, but I'll keep that under wraps for now."

Rico, raising an eyebrow, teased, "Oh, I can't wait to see what surprises you have in store."

I playfully zipped my lips with my fingers, declaring, "Sorry, lips are sealed. You'll just have to wait and see."

Dinner unfolded into a culinary extravaganza with my spotlight on Shrimp Fra Diavolo, a dish swimming in a tantalizing blend of garlicky, spicy tomato sauce. I, the master chef of the evening, revealed the dish's fiery name: "Fra Diavolo." It translates to "brother devil" in Italian, hinting at its bold flavors.

"But fear not," I assured Rico with a playful sparkle in my eye, "I've tailored the spice level to your liking. You'll still savor the essence of virgin olive oil, dried oregano, fire-roasted tomatoes, and Calabrian chili peppers."

As we savored our meal, I shared the story behind my wine selection—a splendid Chianti hailing from my father's homeland in Italy. Our culinary journey began with homemade bruschetta, featuring juicy cherry tomatoes and fragrant basil, drizzled with olive oil and sprinkled with salt, served alongside perfectly grilled baguettes.

Despite the geographical distance, the 2019 Poggerino Nuovo Chianti Classico proved an impeccable choice. It boasted earthy aromas, hints of red fruit, and delicate pepper notes that danced on our palates. The wine complemented every aspect of the meal, from the vibrant bruschetta to the tantalizing Shrimp Fra Diavolo simmering in a rich, garlicky tomato sauce.

The meal culminated in a delightful Italian dessert—Baci gelato adorned with a hazelnut and white chocolate slab—a decadent treat that I proudly presented. "Indulge in this creamy gelato with chocolate and hazelnuts," I proclaimed with an air of confidence, punctuated by a playful Italian accent and a mischievous smile. As we relished each spoonful, I felt a sense of solemnity settle over the room, prompting me to make a heartfelt announcement.

"Rico, I prepared this modest dinner to showcase my culinary skills and reveal a different aspect of myself. However, there are still many layers to my identity that remain unexplored by you."

Rico leaned in attentively, sensing the weight of my words. "Yes, I can cook a little," I confessed, "but there's something else I've been grappling with, something I've never dared to admit until now."

Rico's heart quickened with anticipation; his eyes fixed intently on me.

"I know I'm expected to run the Family Business," I acknowledged, "And while I do want to help transform it into a legitimate enterprise for the benefit of all, that isn't my true passion or life goal."

With bated breath, Rico awaited Tito's revelation. "I want to run a vineyard," I declared, the weight of my confession lifting from my shoulders. "I want to create Tito's Winery."

Rico listened intently, his mind racing with possibilities. After a moment's reflection, he responded with a playful grin, "Tito's and Rico's Winery has a nice ring to it, don't you think?"

My gaze lingered on Rico, a silent invitation shimmering in the depths of his eyes. "I do …I mean …I do think it sounds better with all the added innuendo," I murmured, my words laced with a hint of mischief.

We finished cleaning our meal, put away the dishes, and then decided to spend some time just lying together.

Rico's heart skipped a beat as he met my gaze, feeling the intensity of our connection like a current between us. With a shared laugh, we melted into each other's arms, our bodies igniting with a shared passion that transcended words. Moving to the bedroom, we surrendered to the sensual melody of the music, our movements fluid and instinctive, each touch sparking a wildfire of desire.

As we savored the last drops of Chianti, our lips met in a fervent kiss, leading to enormous pleasure and immense satisfaction. Our bodies danced with desire, each touch igniting sparks of bliss that echoed through the room. With playful whispers and lingering caresses, we explored the depths of our connection, reveling in the intoxicating blend of excitement and intimacy. In the embrace of the night, we surrendered to the timeless allure of love, lost in the euphoria of the moment.

As we remained embraced in the morning light, we both found confidence in each other's presence, a haven from the swirling uncertainties ahead. I grappled with the daunting task of confronting my father, acutely aware of the weight of familial expectations. My will, a constant reminder of my father's authority, cast a shadow over my aspirations.

Yet, despite the daunting odds, I clung to the timeless wisdom of "To thine own self be true," recognizing the imperative of honoring my true desires.

Ever the optimist, Rico offered a glimmer of hope, suggesting we seek Virginia's support first, trusting in her ability to sway my father's opinion. My smile, a reflection of Rico's unwavering support, filled the room with warmth as we embarked on a journey of determination and possibility.

Rico declared his intention to work from home that day, disappearing into the shower to prepare and leaving me to reach for my phone to dial my mother's number. My mom's voice welcomed me on the other end, inquiring about the early call. "Hey there, Mom. Sorry for the early buzz. Rico and I were hoping we might catch up with you today if you're not too busy," I clarified.

Sensing something more, Virginia responded, "Is everything all right, honey? You're not just calling for a chat, are you?" I hesitated, then admitted, "Actually, Mom, I need your advice on something. You know how Dad can be." Virginia, ever the peacemaker, replied, "Of course, darling. I'll be here for you, as always. Why don't we meet for lunch at home? It's as secure as Fort Knox, you know."

I agreed to the plan, setting the time for noon. "Sounds perfect, dear," Virginia affirmed before ending the call with a warm promise. With a smirk, I slipped out of my underwear and into the shower, plotting to give Rico a sudsy surprise that would leave him breathless.

After toweling off, I floated the idea of lunch with my mom, dropping a hint about the property's supposedly impregnable security.

* * * *

Rico

I knew I'd be buried in my work, but reluctantly agreed, masking my true agenda. I didn't want to tip my hand about the logistical insights I'd gleaned during my visit to Saint Vincent de Paul.

Just as I started to find my groove with work, the looming lunch appointment jolted me back to reality, prompting a hurried departure. Upon arrival, we were met with the sight of armed guards discreetly stationed around the property—an ostentatious yet reassuring display of protection orchestrated by the Barbarotti Family. Of course, the Barbarotti's own a security firm with a few inconspicuous family members in crisply pressed uniforms to beef up the surveillance.

Virginia's welcoming presence greeted us at the threshold, her elegance a beacon of warmth. "Well, hello there, my darlings. You both look splendid," she chimed with a twinkle in her eye. Tito couldn't help but praise her, "Mom, you're positively radiant today!"

Me, ever the charmer, added, "Virginia you do look absolutely ravaging!" With a gracious smile, Virginia ushered us inside, assuring us that Salvador was too busy with funeral arrangements.

Navigating to the kitchen, I broached the subject of funeral customs with genuine curiosity. "How do they handle the cremated remains during the Funeral Mass?" I inquired; my tone tinged with respectful intrigue. "I'm not well-versed in Catholic ceremonies, but I've heard they perform the Mass with the presence of the cremated remains. Am I off-base here?"

Virginia's response was a testament to her wisdom. "Ah, the nuances of Catholic rites," she mused, her voice filled with gentle understanding. "Indeed, the Church typically upholds the importance of Funeral Mass rites with the body present. However, in cases where cremation precedes the liturgy, the Mass may proceed in the presence of the cremated remains. As for the particulars of cremations and placement, it's a learning experience for me as well."

Switching gears gracefully, Virginia turned to matters of sustenance with enthusiasm. "Shall we partake in a feast, my dears?" she offered, her eyes shining with intensity. "I've prepared a delightful spread, complete with an array of breads, meats, and fixings. And let's not forget my famous chili—a perfect indulgence for this brisk autumn weather."

In the cozy warmth of the kitchen, plates were filled, and conversation flowed. Sensing my apprehension, Virginia offered words of comfort, her maternal instinct kicking in. "You know, Tito, you can always speak your mind here. Same goes for you, Rico," she reassured us with a gentle smile.

* * * *

Tito

Taking a deep breath, I broached the topic that weighed heavily on my mind. "Mom, remember my trip to northern California last year? I didn't just visit wineries for fun. I was researching, thinking about our family's legacy,"

My voice tinged with determination. "Our roots lie in winemaking, not in the life we've been living. I want to bring that tradition back and make it profitable again. It's a passion of mine, something I know I can succeed in."

Virginia listened attentively; her expression unwavering as I poured out my heart. "Tito, darling, your happiness and success are what matter most to us," she replied, her voice steady. "But timing is everything, and the timing couldn't be any worse especially now with the funeral and the gang troubles looming over us. Let's wait for the right moment when it's safe for everyone. You know if I bring this up with your father now all he will do is say no. We have to be strategic and plan it when the time is right." Virginia's words carried the weight of caution and concern.

Rico, ever the supportive partner, chimed in with understanding. "You're right, Virginia. Tito just needed to get this off his chest, and I stand by him. But we'll bide our time, wait for the storm to pass, you're positively correct," echoing Virginia's sentiments.

I maintained what Rico announced, and with that, Virginia, the consummate hostess, gracefully changed the subject.

"More chili anyone?" With a simple, graceful pivot, Virginia shifted the conversation, her charm as radiant as ever.

We finished our wonderful lunch, which my mom always puts together at the last minute, and as we were leaving, I felt a thousand pounds of weight fall from my shoulders. Finally, I had expressed what I had wanted for so long and felt heard. On the drive home, I reached for Rico's hand to express his gratitude for encouraging me to take the initiative.

Rico responded, "We're here for each other Tito, and I'll do everything to help us find happiness and fulfillment in the life we both deserve."

Rico still had work to attend to, while I mentioned wanting to call the shop where my Tesla was undergoing bodywork to check if it was close to being fixed. Regaining the ability to drive was paramount for me, although I was grateful for Rico's support and the use of his car whenever needed.

As the days dwindled, apprehension hung heavy in the air, culminating with the eve before the Funeral Mass; Rico and I both bore the weight of stress, admittedly for different reasons. I grappled with the daunting task of delivering a eulogy for my Uncle Sully, feeling the pressure to articulate the right words. Memories of babysitting Sully and Maxine's children flooded my mind, adding to my anxiety.

My father, equally burdened, meticulously orchestrated every detail, ensuring flawless execution of the plans and warding off any potential disruptions from the infamous BTF. While Rico navigated the complexities of keeping everything all together as the specter of impending danger loomed.

* * * *

Rico

As the night before the funeral unfolded, I found myself gripped by a sense of foreboding that refused to dissipate. Despite the reassurances from Liz and the other agents stationed inside the church, a knot of anxiety coiled tightly in my stomach.

I received a text message from Liz about rumors of a public hit circulating, casting a shadow of apprehension over the proceedings. Despite the assurances of Agents Liz, Muller, and

Deming stationed inside the church, I remained on edge. Outside, the cavalry stood ready, poised to intercept any unforeseen threats.

The tension was undeniable, impervious to any attempt to dispel it. Every breath seemed to carry the weight of uncertainty, each heartbeat echoing the rhythm of anxious uneasiness. Like an invisible specter, the tension wrapped its tendrils around every soul present, tightening its grip with each passing moment.

It was a tangible presence, almost suffocating in its intensity, casting a shadow over even the most mundane of interactions. Despite everyone's best efforts to push it away, to find solace in distraction, the anxiety lingered as a constant reminder. It was as though the very fabric of reality had been woven with threads of apprehension, binding them all in a web of collective unease.

Yet, beyond the prevailing tension and uncertainty, there was hope for a rainbow, the symbol of hope beyond the storm. Each of us harbored our individual aspirations for a return to normalcy, yearning for the day when the weight of fear and apprehension would lift like a fog dissipating in the morning sun.

* * * *

Tito

Despite the challenges ahead, there was a shared resolve to persevere and navigate the murky waters of adversity with unwavering determination. Everyone held onto the belief that brighter days awaited on the horizon, beckoning us to emerge from the shadows and embrace life once more, renewed and strengthened by the trials we faced.

No one wanted it more than Rico and me. We both clung to a singular dream: to carve out our path in the tranquil vineyards of northern California. Our vision shimmered with the promise of a boutique winery, a sanctuary where we could escape the shadows of our past and embrace the simplicity of a normal life.

With each passing day, the allure of leaving organized crime behind grew stronger, igniting a fervent desire to break free from the shackles of my upbringing. I envisioned a life intertwined with the cutting-edge world of blockchain technology, seeking to transform the family business into a beacon of legitimacy.

My dream is to cultivate a team of innovators united in their mission to revolutionize the agricultural industry. Through transparency and accountability, we aim to modernize the wine business and ensure the seamless distribution of our products. Plus, we wanted to make wine that was really good, too!

CHAPTER 11

Tito

Navigating the intricate maze of emotions surrounding funerals felt like trying to solve a Rubik's Cube with mittens on—a puzzling mix of confusion and frustration with no way to solve grief. Each family member grappled with a spectrum of sentiments and expectations, from overt displays of grief to silent contemplation.

The somber atmosphere enveloped us all, allowing some to openly express our sorrow while others found themselves overwhelmed by emotions long suppressed. Despite the heavy weight of mourning, there lingered a quiet gratitude for the moments of sharing our grief together with family.

The morning passed in a flurry of phone calls with various family members. Each conversation tinged with sorrow and concern. Maxine's voice, heavy with emotion, reached out to Rico and me, requesting that we watch over the boys while she tended to her distress.

Though I readily agreed, Rico couldn't shake his apprehensions about their safety, his mind lingering on the potential threats that still loomed. His familiarity with the criminal psyche made him acutely aware of the dangers, even as I tried to reassure him.

My mom expressed her desire to sit beside me and my dad during the services, while I insisted on having Rico by my other side. After much deliberation, we decided to position the boys between us—a compromise tinged with regret as Rico grappled with concerns about their safety.

As noon approached, Rico and I learned that we would be responsible for the boys during the wake, known as the rosary service. This solemn occasion, where prayers were offered and the rosary recited in honor of the departed, typically took place in a funeral home. However, with Uncle Sully already cremated, they opted to hold it in the prayer room of the church. There, the priest would preside over the vigil service, offering prayers and scripture readings. Though eulogies were customary, it seemed that only Maxine and perhaps a few close friends would deliver them. Virginia had made no mention of joining.

It was already ten A.M., and I had been on the phone since seven A.M., navigating through a flurry of calls. Rico, already showered and shaved, tried to coax me off the phone and into the shower, concerned for my well-being. He swiftly prepared a light breakfast to stabilize my glycemic levels, unwilling to risk me fainting during my eulogy at my family's house after Mass.

After some cajoling, Rico finally persuaded me to clean up and start getting ready. With Maxine set to drop off the boys, Rico ensured we were prepared to keep the boys occupied. Additionally, Rico had some last-minute work stuff he had to do and informed me that he would meet Liz at the church and just wanted to give her a quick call before we headed off to coordinate our preparations.

* * * *

Rico

As everything started to feel overwhelmingly chaotic, the last thing we needed was to add two teenage boys to the mix. Be that as it may, I mirrored Maxine's perspective, reminding myself to consider how he would feel if he were the one grieving. I knew we would navigate through the day, one minute at a time. My first priority was to get Tito ready and fed, then to settle the boys in the den with some video games to keep them occupied until departure time.

Remarkably, everything unfolded exactly as I had envisioned. Tito was finally dressed, and we both enjoyed a breakfast of toasted blueberry waffles topped with fresh blueberries and scrambled eggs. I even whipped up a protein shake blended with frozen mango and other fruits.

The boys arrived without any issues and were introduced to "Uncle Rico"—a title that resonated with me, marking the first time I had ever been referred to as an uncle. Growing up, Tito had taken care of the boys, so they knew they were in for a treat and happily engaged themselves with video games in the den area.

We still had another hour before they needed to head to the church, but I needed to make my call with Liz on her ETA. The ceremony was set for three P.M., and I wanted some time to prepare, as well as to speak with Liz about some work issues.

Tito sat with the boys in the den, giving me some space and the chance to make my call without disturbance. I retreated to the bedroom for privacy, mindful of being overheard.

I called Lieutenant Guild first, who reported that the entire department was abuzz, establishing a meeting point a few blocks away in Lincoln Park from the church. Meanwhile, Homeland Security maintained vigilance at nearby DePaul University, while SWAT remained on standby, poised to intervene at a moment's notice should a hostage situation or similar crisis arise.

I sincerely hoped that such drastic measures wouldn't be necessary. With everything appearing to fall into place, Lieutenant alerted me that Liz had concealed an earpiece beneath her hair to stay informed. The arrangement was to meet her at the church parking lot at 2:30 with both Agent Muller and Agent Deming, allowing ample time for me, Tito, and the boys to arrive and for me to prepare my bulletproof vest and jacket.

Finishing with my calls, I came back out of the bedroom to announce to everyone, "Twenty minutes until departure," directing Tito and the boys to wrap up their gaming session. I quickly ran through a mental checklist of tasks to complete upon reaching the church.

Already in what I referred to as my "Combat Mode," I issued a commanding call for everyone to prepare to depart. "This means bathroom breaks now," I declared firmly, "because you're not getting up during the service. And no more drinking liquids until it's over."

Surprisingly, the two boys, Timothy, and Billy, responded positively to my authoritative tone. I balanced my strictness with affection, ensuring they understood the expectations. I reassured them that after the service, we'd treat them to some frozen yogurt before heading to what the Catholic Church referred to as a *repast*—a gathering after a funeral service, in this case at Tito's parent's house.

While some people called it a reception, Tito explained to me that repasts were generally less formal. Nevertheless, there was a Yoberri Gourmet frozen yogurt place up the street that I had noticed, and I promised to stop there if everyone behaved. With that, the stage was set—the new sheriff was in town.

Tito responded to my sudden leadership role with a quip, "Guess we know who wears the pants in this family."

I chuckled, replying, "Ha ha, I just want to make sure everything goes perfectly, that's all."

Tito raised his hand mockingly, saying, "Amen to that, brother!"

We were all prepared as I ordered, "Everyone carry their own jackets to keep them from getting wrinkled. Once we get to the parking lot, give me a moment to put mine on in the church bathroom. I just need to find my friend, Liz, so Timothy and Billy stay close to your Uncle Tito! Understood?"

It was a rhetorical question, of course. The drive to the church parking lot at 2:30 was smooth, taking less than fifteen minutes. We arrived a bit early, and Liz was already there as I excused myself and asked Tito to wait for me before entering.

My eyes scanned the area for anything out of the ordinary, noticing the other two agents talking to Liz, as I headed their way.

"Hey, is everything ready?" I didn't pause for small talk; I remained in command mode.

Liz replied, "We're all set, and everything is in place. Lt. Guild ensured the church was swept, and all attendees were screened. Nothing out of the ordinary."

"Good," I replied briskly. "Just let me run to the restroom to put on my vest and jacket…you all are wearing one, correct?"

Everyone nodded, and I couldn't help but suppress a chuckle at the mental image of bulletproof vests under the agents' Catholic white robes as they attempted to blend into the clergy for the mass. Shaking off the absurd vision, I jogged into the church restroom, returning minutes later with my jacket on, looking considerably sharper.

Liz remarked, "You clean up well, Agent Bass."

I offered a grateful smile, my mind already preoccupied with the possibility of forgetting something.

I announced, "Well, everyone, it's time for the funeral. Please stay alert. The average length of a Catholic funeral Mass is typically around one hour, but this can vary. Are there any questions?"

Everyone looked at me, impressed by my professionalism, and the three agents maintained their composure.

The boys and Tito watched as I made his way back over to them, observing as other cars lined up in the parking lot. "Let's all head into the church before the aisles get too crowded," I announced.

Tito responded, "Yes, sir!" and the boys, playing along with their uncles, saluted Rico with a resounding, "Yes, Sir!"

I smiled; I already had a fondness for the boys as I started reciting, "Hup, one, two, three. Hup, one, two, three," but now my focus shifted to sweeping the church with my eyes.

Offering a general warning, I advised Tito to be cautious and vigilant for anything out of the ordinary.

Perplexed, he inquired, "What do you mean?"

I replied, "You know…the BTF group or something."

Tito reassured me, "I talked to my dad, and he assured me he has security in place. Any attempt by the BTF would be foolish."

I replied solemnly, "I hope you're right Tito, and nothing happens. But remember, we also didn't anticipate your house blowing up. So, please, do me a favor and keep your eyes open."

Tito noticed how nicely everyone was dressed as they were getting out of their cars. He recited the proper etiquette for a Catholic Mass to me and the boys, "Everyone should arrive dressed in somber attire, adhering to the tradition of wearing black or dark colors at a funeral."

Continuing, he clarified, "Since this is your first time attending a Catholic funeral mass, there are certain customs to expect. Respectful attire is paramount, emphasizing modesty and avoiding overly casual or revealing clothing. Throughout the mass, attendees are expected to follow the cues of the priest, standing, and sitting as indicated. This ritualistic participation is a hallmark of Catholic masses, including funerals."

It took approximately thirty minutes for everyone to find their seats in the packed church. Tito added, "Tardiness to a mass, especially a funeral mass, is considered disrespectful."

I gave him a dirty look as if to say, "Well, certainly not us, because we got here early!"

The Mass commenced with the Opening Rites, marked by the entrance of the priest and other participants. Following this, the priest greeted the congregation and led them in an opening prayer.

Tito cautioned me, "Be prepared for frequent changes in posture, including standing, sitting, and kneeling for prayer. You'll also be expected to participate in various prayers and responses, as well as sing hymns. If you're unfamiliar with the prayers or hymns, you can simply listen and follow along. There is also an itinerary and songbooks in the pews for reference, but singing is optional."

I took everything that Tito told me in stride and casually glanced back to ensure everyone was seated, noting only familiar faces. Liz was sitting on the other side of me as she whispered to the Lieutenant that everything was proceeding smoothly. At the back of the church, a balcony housed the organist, whose music resonated throughout the sanctuary, especially the deep bass notes that seemed to shake one's very soul. While many turned to acknowledge the organ playing, my gaze lingered, scanning the balcony for any signs of disturbance, but all appeared in order. After a series of prayers, the Opening Rites concluded, transitioning into the Liturgy of the Word.

Tito remained stoic and watched everything going on with the service, mostly feeling numb. I referenced the itinerary he found in the pew. This segment, central to the Catholic funeral mass, featured readings from the Bible chosen to reflect on the life of the deceased, accompanied by a homily delivered by the priest.

As attendees directed their attention to the urn positioned in the center of the room, I couldn't help but marvel at the majestic marble altar adorned with intricate carvings. It was further accentuated by beautiful wreaths and peace lilies, casting an ethereal aura throughout the church.

While everything seemed to proceed smoothly, I remained vigilant, unwilling to take any chances. As I watched Tito, I thought some might perceive me as overly fidgety, but I was determined to make sure that I and the rest of the family remained safe. Though I felt Tito's parents' security had everything under control, I still was not at ease.

I knew how structured the funeral Mass would be, and it just seemed to drag on. The Liturgy of the Eucharist followed, accompanied by hymns and the reverberating organ, which I think they put in just to shake people awake. This segment of the Catholic funeral Mass involves the consecration of bread and wine by the priest, who then offers the Eucharist to the congregation. For practicing Catholics like some of Tito's family members, partaking in the sacrament is customary, as in any other mass.

However, Tito only came to church for weddings and funerals. I'm not a practicing Catholic, and neither is Liz. So, we were not obliged, didn't participate, and remained seated. We watched as the boys went up and immediately came back once they received their sacrament. I scanned both sides of the church and asked Liz if she noticed anything unusual. She shook her head no and dared not talk during the service.

The Mass had been going on for over forty-five minutes so far without a hitch. I thought to myself, "We're in the home stretch, and maybe the BTF had gotten word that the Barbarotti Family was planning to put a hit on all of them." Regardless, I remained vigilant.

Tito knew we didn't have much more to go, but he also realized he would soon be asked to read a Scripture passage that his parents and Maxine had requested.

As the Mass drew to a close, only the Closing Rites remained. In Catholic funeral ceremonies, these rites typically entail a prayer of commendation and a final blessing from the priest, followed by a recessional hymn. Despite the absence of eulogies during the service and no spoken tributes, Tito informed me that he would have the opportunity to deliver his eulogy later at the house.

However, Tito's nerves were on edge as he waited for his turn to recite the Scripture. Each passing moment felt like an eternity, his heart was so loud I feared it might drown out the priest's voice. Tito had rehearsed the Scripture passage countless times, but now, as the priest called him forward, his palms grew clammy, and he told me his legs felt like lead.

Most people didn't even notice him get up as the solemn Mass stretched on, fatigue began to settle over some attendees, lulling them into a drowsy state. Just when it seemed that slumber might claim the whole congregation, Tito adjusted the microphone, making a high-pitched squeal, startling the organist who accidentally stepped on the organ's pedals with a haunting chord that echoed through the church, jolting me to attention. My gaze snapped toward the source, only to freeze in horror at the sight of a dark figure looming in front of the organist.

Instinct surged through me, as I propelled myself into action and swiftly retrieved my gun from its concealed holster. With adrenaline coursing through my veins, I leaped to my feet and sprinted toward Tito, who was oblivious to what was going on.

Suddenly, my voice cut through the air like a blade, commanding attention and sparking panic among the congregation. "Shooter In the Balcony!" The chaos was immediate, confusion and fear spreading like wildfire as my warning ignited panic throughout the church.

In a frantic blur, chaos erupted as I lunged in front of Tito, getting off one shot and shielding him from harm as the assailant returned fire. I felt a piercing sting, and suddenly nothing.

Screams and shots pierced the air, mingling with Liz's yelling instructions for everyone to seek cover.

Amidst the pandemonium, the organists panicked and dove onto the pedals of the organ disrupting and unleashing a discordant symphony of deep, ominous tones that reverberated through the church, mirroring the violence unfolding within its walls.

Suddenly, a chilling cry shattered the chaos, echoing through the sanctuary: "He's been hit."

* * * *

Tito

I noticed Liz racing in my direction as she struggled to discern who the shooter was, her eyes darting between Rico and the shadowy figure on the balcony. Rico lay motionless before the lectern, right in front of me, as my anguished cries filled the air while I knelt by his side.

Members of my family sprang into action, ushering Salvador and Virginia to safety as I cradled Rico in my arms, my tears mingling with my lover's blood. Time seemed to stand still as the FBI descended upon the scene, their swift actions punctuated by the arrival of paramedics who rushed to Rico's aid.

As they wheeled Rico away on a gurney, my world began to collapse. Every event was going through rewind like my panicked cries reverberating off the walls, blending with the piercing sirens outside.

Liz's words broke through the mayhem, shattering my illusion, "Rico is an FBI agent and he'll get the best doctors to work on him."

Shock washed over me, a tsunami of disbelief crashing down, as I watched Rico disappear into the ambulance, his form fleeting like a fading dream. My mind just couldn't handle the sudden turn of events, a cyclone of confusion and disbelief engulfing my thoughts. "Rico is an FBI agent," played over and over again in my head.

Numbness turned into rigor mortis, every muscle stiffening with the weight of the truth. The cacophony of screams and shouts became a symphony of confusion, each note playing out in discordant harmony. Emergency lights flashed blindingly bright, casting stark shadows that danced eerily across the church walls. The pungent scent of blood mingled with the sharp tang of disinfectant, assaulting my senses and threatening to overwhelm me.

A knot of nausea twisted in my stomach, threatening to spill its contents as I struggled to draw breath into lungs that felt as though they were being crushed by an invisible vice. At that moment, I felt as though I were trapped in a nightmare, unable to wake up or escape the horrors unfolding before me.

Every fiber of my being screamed for action, for movement, for escape. Yet, I remained frozen in place, paralyzed by the enormity of the situation. Time seemed to stretch and warp, each second dragging on interminably as I grappled with the reality of Rico's betrayal and the chaos that now surrounded us.

I tried to cope with a maelstrom of conflicting emotions—betrayal mingled with gratitude, leaving me feeling adrift and isolated. With Rico wounded and possibly dead, I felt a profound sense of abandonment, compounded by the absence of my parents.

As the bedlam unfolded, I wandered aimlessly in despair and was noticed by the priest who had presided over the Funeral Mass liturgy.

Sensing my confusion, the priest offered words of comfort, suggesting that it was part of God's plan to spare my life and that greater things awaited me. He encouraged me to open my heart to God, assuring me that I would be guided on my path.

I blurted out, "The only path I feel is the one of total havoc on a train from hell and all I want to do is to get off and go home.

Liz glanced at me, assessing my condition, but her attention quickly shifted as she set off to locate the two missing priests. It dawned on me then that Liz must be an FBI agent, too, and those priests Rico spoke to earlier were likely undercover agents as well.

As Liz combed through the church property, she suddenly shouted, "I found them, they're alive." To their astonishment, they discovered the priests knocked out and bound with zip ties in the Sacristy, a concealed room behind the west side of the sanctuary.

Amidst the echoes in the church, I caught Liz's words, "The assailant managed to infiltrate undetected, lurking in hiding throughout the extensive property. Unbeknownst to us, the church harbored numerous secret areas, proving to be the downfall of the entire operation." She added, "Despite the chaos, I hope Agent Bass, my colleague Rico, is okay. It seems he hit his head hard, and even with a bulletproof vest, there could still be significant damage."

I stood next to the priest, speechless, pondering, "How did this happen? How could I have been so blind?"

* * * *

Tito's Family Home

Salvador and Virginia Barbarotti arrived at their home just a few blocks away, while the other security van, carrying Maxine and her boys, also pulled up. As they disembarked, Virginia anxiously inquired, "Where's the other van with Tito?"

Sal's grim response echoed through the tense air, "There are only two vans."

Virginia erupted into a frenzy, her voice echoing with fear and frustration, "How the hell could you leave Tito there!" Her outburst reverberated through the neighborhood, a testament to the panic and urgency of the situation.

Sal realized, with a sinking feeling, surrounded by the frenzy and disorder, that they had overlooked Tito. Hastily, he ordered the security service to backtrack and retrieve him.

Virginia, overcome with emotion, collapses into tears, the weight of the situation and Rico's selfless act to save her son crashing down upon her. All she wanted now was to locate her son and rush to the hospital to find out about Rico's condition.

* * * *

Northwestern Memorial Hospital

Rico lay unconscious as the ambulance arrived at Northwestern Memorial Hospital in Chicago, known as one of the best in the country. He was shot in the side chest area, but the bullet did not penetrate due to the vest he was wearing. The paramedics assessed that he probably had a few broken ribs and as he jumped in front of the speaker, he ended up landing head-first onto a marble bench that was just to the side.

He had a gaping wound to his head and that is where the blood came from. He was still unconscious, and they wanted him up to get an MRI right away to see what damage had occurred. No one followed him to the hospital. He was all alone. The hospital staff nurses were trying to get ahold of the next of kin, but all they knew was that he was an FBI agent. Nothing more.

* * * *

Liz Doucet

Liz was still at the church, trying to manage everything amidst the chaos surrounding her. "I made sure that the paramedics and another ambulance would transport Agent Murry and Agent Deming to the same hospital as Agent Bass," she said. "They're conscious now and provided details of how they were overwhelmed and blindsided by the assailant."

When other FBI agents asked where the assailant came from, Liz responded as best as she could, "Where he came from? No one has a clue yet, but he was in the church before we arrived. He managed to get up to the organ balcony where they suspected he had hidden a sharp-shooting rifle."

Liz continued to recount the events, "The organist also sustained slight injuries when he dived underneath the organ and hit his head. The paramedics bandaged his forehead, and he was advised to watch out for a possible concussion and go to the hospital if needed."

While surveying the scene at the church and its once-ordinary parking lot, which has now transformed into a bustling nerve center for law enforcement operations, Liz noted the significant progress made in the investigation.

As she received updates from the earbuds she was still wearing and remained in touch with Lt. Guild, Liz informed the other agents, "Agent Bass's appeal to Lt. Guild for access to Luther Hoop, a high-ranking figure in the Gangster Collection, proved fruitful. Critical intelligence was obtained regarding the activities of the Bad Town Faction, including gun trafficking and human smuggling enterprises."

She said, "Luther provided valuable insights into their operational hub: a warehouse located in the industrial precincts of the South Side along Stony Island Avenue. Collaborating with the Chicago SWAT team, the FBI initiated surveillance on the facility, uncovering a gathering of key figures orchestrating the day's events and planning further criminal activities. One figure they noticed who was familiar to them was none other than Ronnie Barbarotti."

Liz relayed the information to Lt. Guild, who exclaimed in disbelief, "What the hell is he doing there?"

"Currently," Liz reported, "the SWAT team is poised for action pending Guild's authorization. The lieutenant has swiftly sanctioned the operation, underscoring the urgency and magnitude of the problem. His decision was critically fueled by the newfound intelligence provided by Luther Hoop and the FBI."

She shared the latest update in a concerned tone: "Agent Bass, Agent Muller, and Agent Deming have all been hospitalized. However, the task force has taken swift action and is working on dismantling the criminal network that has been operating out of the BTF facility. The raid is still ongoing, and Lt. Guild is determined to uncover the truth behind Ronnie Barbarotti's unexpected presence. This confrontation will be a high-stakes one, and it will hopefully resolve all the lingering questions."

* * * *

Tito

Suddenly, my father's security van screeched into the parking lot, and I was gently ushered inside, still visibly in shock. Without asking for details, the priest who was still with me bid me farewell, and I was taken to my parents' house, grateful for one thing—heading home.

Upon arriving, my mother, Virginia, rushed over, her emotions unmistakable. She enveloped me in a tight embrace, tears streaming down her face as she uttered, "We're so sorry, son…we never meant to leave you…We're so sorry about Rico, and we want to take you to the hospital to see how he is."

Still in a daze, I shocked my mother by saying, "No, I don't want to see him. I don't even know who he is."

Realizing the depth of my pain, Virginia gently replied, "Of course, you know who he is, son. He is the man who loves you, and whom you love. I realize you didn't know he was an FBI agent, but your father and I knew it all along. We didn't tell you right away because we knew he would protect you, and that is exactly what he did, son."

I gave my mother a look of disbelief. "It's all too much for me to digest."

My heart felt like a stormy sea, tossing, and turning with emotions too raw to contain. I gently pushed my mom away, the echo of my footsteps reverberating through the empty hallway as I retreated to my childhood room. My voice trembled with uncertainty as I uttered, "I don't know who to trust anymore."

Despite the swirling revelations, my mind remained surprisingly clear. However, rationality struggled to make sense of an irrational situation.

Salvatore, observing the scene, approached my mom to offer comfort. "He'll be okay, just give him some time. He feels betrayed, but he just needs to realize everything we did, and even what Rico did, was for his own safety. Love always wins out in the end." Such profound words coming from a Mafia Boss; who would've known?

In the days following Rico's shooting, I found myself ensnared in the depths of conflicting emotions. The revelation of Rico's identity as an FBI agent had shaken me to the core, leaving me still grappling with a profound sense of distrust. Each passing moment seemed to amplify the weight of this truth, casting a shadow over our once-idyllic relationship.

In the quiet moments of reflection, I found myself wrestling with a myriad of emotions, trying to untangle the threads of confusion and uncertainty that seemed to embroil my thoughts. As I replayed the memories we shared, I searched for clues I might have overlooked, a glimpse of the hidden truths Rico carried with him.

In the face of turbulence, one undeniable fact emerged: Rico's willingness to risk everything to save me resonated deeply with my core, a sacrifice that I couldn't ignore, no matter how much I struggled to come to terms with all that had happened.

I pondered the resilience of our love, wondering if it could weather the storm that threatened to tear us apart. Though our journey lay ahead, shrouded in uncertainty, I clung to the glimmer of hope that we could emerge from this trial stronger, our bond tempered by the fires of adversity. And perhaps, in the quiet moments of contemplation, I began to entertain the notion that Rico's secrecy stemmed not from deceit, but from a profound desire to shield me from harm.

It was a time of introspection, a journey into the depths of my heart, where I found solace in the realization that Rico's unwavering commitment and selfless bravery were testaments to our connection. In my heart, I discovered a profound reservoir of true love and dedication, one that propelled me forward without hesitation, driven by a selfless determination to protect what I held dear—Rico's love.

CHAPTER 12

One month later

Rico

In the serene confines of my apartment, bathed in the soft glow of evening light, I diligently packed my belongings, the echoes of recent turmoil still reverberating within me. Despite the physical reminders of my recent injuries—my ribs tender, my head now free of its lingering concussion—I found solace in the quiet routine of folding clothes and gathering essentials. Yet, within the tranquility of the moment, my thoughts drifted back to the dismantling of the task force and the pivotal strides made in catching and exposing the illegal actions of the Bad Town Faction.

The revelation that shocked few in the Barbarotti Family was the entanglement of Tito's Uncle Ronnie with the BTF. He devised a reckless scheme, and Uncle Sully got tricked into helping him, betraying their own kin by peddling illegal firearms and narcotics in collaboration with the BTF. Unbeknownst to the two uncles, the BTF harbored deeper, more sinister intentions. Their alliance was a facade for a treacherous plot to infiltrate and dismantle the Barbarotti Family, seizing control of Chicago's underworld. Fortunately, their clandestine double-dealings were brought to light, thwarting their grandiose ambitions, and exposing their duplicitous nature.

The BTF's nefarious operations had been laid bare, their members apprehended, and their criminal empire crumbling. I reflected on the justice served: two members were shot dead during the raid, plus the assassin that I shot dead in the church, the rest facing life sentences for their myriad crimes. Racketeering, gunrunning, human trafficking, and migrant smuggling, alongside charges of attempted murder and murder-for-hire, had led to their downfall.

Tito's Uncle Ronnie, too, received a ten-year sentence for gun and drug trafficking. As the black sheep of the Barbarotti Family, he was given a chance to reflect during his time in prison, a sentence that Sal, the head of the family, had yet to address. For Ronnie, prison life was perhaps the best option, and he accepted his punishment without appeal or resistance.

After the dust settled, my noble service did not go unnoticed. I was awarded the prestigious FBI Medal for Meritorious Achievement, a testament to my unwavering dedication and courage in the face of insurmountable challenges. This honor was more than just a medal; it symbolized profound gratitude for my extraordinary contributions to national security and the relentless pursuit of justice.

As I methodically sorted through my possessions, a heavy burden weighed upon me, one that no amount of physical healing could alleviate. With each fold of fabric, each item placed into a suitcase, I couldn't shake the persistent ache of regret gnawing at my core. I replayed countless scenarios in my mind, grappling with the question of whether I could have acted differently, sparing Tito from doubt and uncertainty. I was haunted by the knowledge that my silence about my true identity as an FBI agent had sown seeds of mistrust, overshadowing the relief of saving Tito's life. Though my intentions had been noble, driven by a desire to shield Tito and maintain the element of surprise, I found myself ensnared in a web of remorse, wrestling with the unintended consequences of my actions.

By the same token, I reflected on all I had accomplished, carefully evaluating each event in my mind. My undercover work had been instrumental in cracking the case wide open, providing me with invaluable insight that no other FBI agent could have obtained. Yet, I couldn't shake the nagging question: how could I have foreseen falling in love with the son of a notorious Mob Boss? Despite my doubts, I realized the importance of not being too hard on myself. Life was about taking risks and sometimes letting the pieces fall where they may, knowing that, ultimately, I had acted in the best interests of all involved.

As I stood by the window of my apartment, the dwindling light of dusk painted the room in a kaleidoscope of colors, casting a spell of nostalgia and contemplation. Yet, beneath the soft hues of the setting sun, a biting chill crept in, the icy fingers of winter tightening their grip with each passing moment. Despite the vibrant display outside, the air grew colder by the minute, a stark reminder of the impending winter's embrace. With each item now carefully packed away, I felt the weight of the past months lift, replaced by a sense of closure and newfound freedom.

Time seemed to have whisked by, leaving behind cherished memories to overshadow any lingering doubts. This realization healed not only my body but also my heart, filling me with newfound hope and a profound sense of gratitude for the power of love to transcend adversity and bring about transformative change.

I would attend the Christmas party at the Barbarotti residence tonight, a gathering that held both anticipation and apprehension for me. It marked my return to the familiar yet changed surroundings since the tumultuous events of the recent past. What would they think of me, and would they appreciate what I did to save Tito's life? Despite the memories flooding back, some details remained fuzzy, but I knew what was in my heart and was determined to fight for it.

While I finished folding my clothes and sorting through my belongings, vivid memories resurfaced. I recalled the days of unconsciousness, the challenging journey to recover my strength and faculties. These memories merged with the fog of amnesia, obscuring some details while others remained vivid. Each day brought new recollections, shedding light on moments once lost in the haze of trauma. Now, it was time for me to move on and embrace a fresh start. With resolve, I gathered my suitcases, cast a final glance around the apartment, dropped the keys on the kitchen counter, and headed out to the elevator, knowing I was closing the door on this chapter of my life for good.

As consciousness slowly returned to me, I found myself greeted by the reassuring presence of Tito, steadfast beside me. Our bond weathered the storms of suffering, transcending the confines of time and memory. It was Tito's presence that brought me the power to forgive myself—a balm to my wounded spirit. Yet, it came with an unspoken understanding, a silent pact born of shared trials and unspoken fears. I sensed the weight of Tito's expectations and his earnest plea, a constant reminder of the value of transparency and the gravity of truth: to "Never, Ever, ever!" conceal important information from him again.

I grasped the weighty significance of Tito's desires, embracing the commitment with unwavering dedication. With every fiber of my being, I pledged to traverse the intricate pathways of our shared fate, promising to disclose all, whether it be moments of joy or shadows of pain.

I had harbored the desire to disclose everything to Tito from the outset, yet I couldn't risk jeopardizing the investigation or the expectations of the task force. However, circumstances had shifted, and now my priority was clear.

At the tender age of twenty-four, my promising career with the FBI had come to an abrupt and harrowing end. The gunshot wound and severe head injury I sustained plunged me into a dark abyss of uncertainty and pain, leaving me hospitalized for weeks with amnesia and PTSD. Despite my relatively short tenure as a criminal psychologist, the perils of the job had exacted a devastating toll on my young life. My resignation from the bureau served as a stark reminder of the inherent dangers lurking within law enforcement, no matter one's level of experience. With a heavy heart, I faced an uncertain future, grappling with the physical and psychological scars that would forever alter the course of my destiny.

Tito would become my full-time focus now. Plans were in motion for us to depart shortly after the Christmas party, heading for Sonoma, California. In heartfelt conversations with his father, Tito had asserted his autonomy and vision for the future of the Barbarotti Family organization. After the turbulent events they'd weathered, Sal finally recognized Tito's right to shape his own destiny.

In the aftermath of the Bad Town Faction's demise, the Barbarotti Family found themselves at a crossroads, with the once imminent threat now vanquished. As the dust settled, attention turned to the North Side of Chicago, where new challenges awaited. With a strategic shift towards legitimacy and respectability, the dawn of the New Family Plan emerged, ushering in a new era under Salvatore Barbarotti's visionary leadership.

No longer shackled by the moniker of "Greasy Hands Salv," he embraced his role as a shrewd businessman, propelled by the transformative vision of his son, Tito. Together, they embarked on the arduous journey of sowing the seeds of change, forging a path towards a brighter, more prosperous future for the Barbarotti empire, with no room for the likes of anyone like Ronnie, whom Sal decided to disown from the entire family. Sal's last comment on the matter was, "May Ronnie rot in jail!" as he flicked his cigar into the ashtray, his eyes gleaming with resolve.

Tito envisioned a dual role in overseeing the family business's digital transformation while nurturing his aspiration of owning a vineyard. With ambitions aligned, Tito aimed to infuse fresh energy into the organization by empowering a younger generation to take the reins.

Our relocation to California held promise, with familial ties already established in the wine country. Tito's father had a cousin who owned a vineyard in Sonoma, laying the groundwork for their venture into the wine industry.

Tito's expectations flowed like a fine vintage as he envisioned himself immersed in the timeless art of viticulture, ready to drink in every drop of knowledge and refine his skills. He understood that to create a thriving winery, he needed to cultivate not just grapes, but also his expertise as a vintner. While his business acumen was undeniable, Tito recognized the importance of mastering the nuances of winemaking to surround himself with the best in the industry.

If Tito and I were to carve out a legacy, we needed to grasp the essence of what makes a winery and our wines truly exceptional. With each step into this new frontier, I stood as a fearless beacon of support, unwavering in my belief that Tito's potential knew no bounds. Together, we ventured forth, our bond as unyielding as the vines we hoped would one day yield the sweetest fruits of success.

I, currently on a sabbatical due to my disability, found myself on the brink of a significant transformation, eagerly anticipating the forthcoming shift in my academic endeavors. My gaze turned from the shadowed corridors of criminal psychology to the sun-drenched vineyards of enology. With a thirst for knowledge as insatiable as parched earth after rain, I embarked on a journey to unravel the mysteries of wine's psyche. Delving deep into its essence, I sought to decode the enigmatic language of flavor, peeling back the layers of its complexity to reveal the intricate essence woven from the grape's nectar.

It seemed an ideal perspective, offering a tranquil and safe job environment except for the occasional challenge akin to dealing with "sour grapes." All joking aside, I envisioned a fresh path ahead, with Tito as my steadfast companion.

In this pursuit, I aimed to decipher not just the taste, but the very soul of wine, exploring its depths for the hidden truths and whispered secrets that lay dormant within each bottle, waiting to be discovered by those with the patience to listen and the wisdom to discern. In my pursuit of wine's secrets, I aimed to uncover the intricate parallels between wine and human life.

With every swirl of the glass, from the robust richness of Cabernet Sauvignon and the velvety smoothness of Merlot to the delicate floral notes of Chardonnay and the vibrant fruitiness of Pinot Grigio, I envisioned a dance of emotions—love, desire, redemption—playing out in the depths of each sip. Through the varied flavors and textures of wines spanning the spectrum, I sought to reveal a zest of human experience squeezed into each and every drop.

* * * *

As I readied myself for the Christmas party, a sense of expectation tingled in the frosty air. The biting cold of the night promised to deepen, its icy grip tightening with each passing hour. I layered up, bundling myself against the chill that seeped through every crevice, a reminder of the unforgiving nature of winter in Chicago. The lake's frigid waters, now frozen in motion, served as a stark reminder of the raw power of nature, its relentless force capable of freezing even the mightiest waves.

I shuddered at the thought, feeling the bitter winds piercing me like icy daggers. Yet, underneath the bone-chilling cold, I discovered that my heart burned with the warmth of anticipation, the promise of reuniting with Tito fueling my resolve to brave the elements. With a final adjustment of my scarf and a deep breath, I stepped out into the night, ready to face whatever the evening held in store.

Arriving at the Barbarotti Estate, I was greeted at the door by none other than Virginia, who immediately enveloped me in a warm hug of greeting. She welcomed me inside and remarked on how wonderful I looked.

"Besides absolutely looking handsome as ever, you seem well-rested and, umm," Virginia hesitated, searching for the right word. "Happy," she finally said with a smile.

Entering the home, I was engulfed by laughter and camaraderie. I felt a sense of belonging wash over me. I let Virginia know, "No matter how cold the world outside might be, I knew I would always find warmth here in the comfort and company of loved ones."

Virginia's happiness radiated as she expressed, "Well, it is always a joy having you here Rico, especially now for the holiday festivities."

The warmth emanating from the grand mansion wrapped around me like a comforting embrace, banishing the last traces of cold from my bones. As I made my way inside, the festive atmosphere caressed me, transporting me to a world of holiday cheer and merriment.

Fascinated by the twinkling lights and cheerful chatter, I found myself surrounded by the warmth of friendship and the joy of shared moments. The scent of freshly baked cookies and mulled wine mingled with the soft strains of holiday music, creating an ambiance of sheer delight. My heart swelled with gratitude as I took in the scene before me.

The family room buzzed with animated conversations and laughter, imbued with the comforting scent of holiday spices. The Christmas tree towered majestically, its branches adorned with an array of crystal ornaments that caught the light, casting shimmering reflections of silver, gold, and red throughout the room.

Virginia's voice cut through the lively atmosphere. "Oh, by the way, Tito will be arriving shortly. He told me he forgot something important." Her words were punctuated by the optimism of the gathering.

As I stepped into the family room, the warmth of familial love startled me, manifesting in the thunderous applause and heartfelt expressions of gratitude from the Barbarotti Family members. Overwhelmed by emotion, I found myself speechless, my heart swelling with gratitude and affection for the Barbarotti Family.

I stood momentarily dazed in the face of such warmth and acknowledgment, but gathered my thoughts and found the strength to express the depth of my commitment. "I did what I had to," I began, my voice steady despite the swell of emotion in my chest. "Because I knew, without a doubt, that Tito would do the same for me."

* * * *

Tito

As the room collectively basked in appreciation, I made my grand entrance. Adding to the loud applause, I announced, "Here, here!" drawing Rico's gaze with an affectionate smile. With a gentle kiss, I wrapped my arms around Rico, my embrace conveying a depth of affection and gratitude beyond words.

"You are my rock, Rico," I murmured softly, the warmth of my voice comforted Rico like a familiar song. With a subtle gesture, I signaled for silence, my eyes gleaming with promise, hinting that I had something special to share.

Radiating with exuberance, my voice resonated in the room as I began my heartfelt speech.

"My dear friends and family, without this man beside me, I wouldn't be standing here today," I began, my words carrying the weight of sincere thanks. "From the moment I met Rico, I knew there was something extraordinary about him. Though his charm and good looks initially caught my eye, it was his heart that truly captured mine."

I cleared my voice as I continued, "Before the funeral, we shared laughs over the whimsical notion of launching 'Tito's and Rico's Winery'—a lighthearted fantasy that has evolved into a compelling vision of destiny. Now, in the wake of recent events, that dream resonates with newfound clarity and purpose.

I believe, now more than ever, that we possess the grit, determination, and unwavering support of each other needed to turn that dream into a reality. With each step forward, guided by our shared commitment and unwavering resolve, I am confident that together, Rico and I can bring this vision to fruition."

As I continued, my voice quivered with emotion, my gaze unwaveringly fixed on Rico. "Rico is my champion, my guiding light, who brings out the best in me. He's the one who encourages me to be true to myself and to strive for greatness. Today, I stand before you, ready to take the next step in our journey together."

With a flourish of affection, I gracefully descended to one knee, the weight of my deepest feelings instilling the gesture with profound significance. The room fell into a hushed silence, every breath suspended in anticipation, as if the very air itself awaited the next heartbeat.

"I almost forgot to bring this and that's why I'm late, but Rico I have something for you."

There, bathed in the soft, twinkling light reflected off the Christmas tree's shimmering ornaments, I presented a magnificent ring. Its facets glowed with a mesmerizing luster, reflecting the sparkle in Rico's eyes.

Gasps and whispers filled the air as my heartfelt proposal hung in the room, palpably electric with anticipation. Breaking the silence, my voice trembled with vulnerability as I asked Rico the question I had wanted to ask him for a long time.

"Rico," I began, my voice teeming with emotion, "Would you please make me the happiest man on this planet by being my husband and partner in life?"

The room continued holding its breath, tension hanging heavy in the air as all eyes turned to Rico. Overwhelmed with excitement, Rico's heart swelled with love for the man before him.

His voice, though soft, carried the weight of a lifetime's worth of affection and devotion as he responded, "I would love to spend the rest of my life with you as my husband … I love you, Tito!"

As my words echoed through the room, tears of joy glistened in Rico's eyes, my love for him shining brightly for all to see. The moment was electric, charged with the raw emotion of two souls intertwining in a promise of eternal love and commitment.

Laughter and applause filled the air, mingling with overflowing happiness that seemed to dance around the room. As Rico proudly showed off the ring in a dazzling display, the atmosphere crackled with the energy of pure joy and delight.

Salvador and Virginia, their faces radiant with pride and happiness, stood hand in hand, their hearts brimming with love. "Bring out the champagne for a toast," Virginia declared, her voice filled with warmth and affection. Glasses of bubbly were passed around; each sip a symbol of the new beginnings unfolding before them. Applause erupted again, mingling with the sound of clinking glasses as champagne flowed freely.

"We welcome you to the Barbarotti Family, Rico," Virginia proclaimed, her eyes glistening with tears of joy. "You are one of us now, and we couldn't be happier to have you."

Sal, standing tall beside her, added his voice to hers. "Rico, there's no one I'd be prouder to call my son-in-law than you," he declared, his tone filled with genuine affection. "I love you as if you were already my very own son."

Surrounded by laughter and all the toasting glasses, Rico felt as if he had finally found his place in the world. He raised his glass in a silent toast, his heart swarming with gratitude for the love and acceptance surrounding him. This moment marked not just the beginning of a new chapter, but the start of a new adventure filled with love, joy, and endless possibilities.

Rico desired a moment alone, prompting him to grab me and discreetly slip away from the bustling gathering. Guided by the faint sounds of laughter and conversation, we navigated through the throng of guests until we reached the kitchen. Here, our secluded haven muffled the noise from the festivities, we finally found ourselves alone shielded by the sturdy walls and closed door. In this sanctuary of privacy, Rico poured out his heart to me, his voice infused with sincerity and unwavering devotion.

"Tito, you've brought an abundance of joy into my life," he confessed, his eyes alight with love. "I'm so excited to begin our new journey together." With an earnest embrace, Rico believed that every trial we faced had only strengthened the bond between us.

Agreeing with Rico, I met his gaze with unwavering trust. "I trust you because I know your heart, Rico, and I know you always have our best interests in mind," I said, my voice filled with unwavering confidence. Our bond felt unbreakable at that moment, strengthened by our shared drive and mutual loyalty. Rico felt a surge of gratitude for my trust, knowing that we could face any challenge together with such unwavering faith.

Encouraged by my pledge, Rico broached the topic we had both been eagerly anticipating. "So, when and where shall we tie the knot?" he inquired, eager to hear my vision.

Lost in thought, I painted a vivid picture of our dream wedding, "An idyllic vineyard setting with rolling hills, an alfresco celebration beneath the shade of ancient oak trees, and the sounds of a string quartet filling the air. I envision a perfect early summer's day, perhaps at the start of June," I mused.

Rico couldn't help but be enchanted by my vision. "I love your style," he whispered, drawing closer, "Add a band we can dance to after the ceremony, and we've got a plan."

After the party ended, Rico mentioned to me, "I'm all packed and ready to go, but I've got nowhere to sleep tonight."

I fiashed my signature sly smile, replying, "Oh, you're staying here with me. We can finish packing together before we head off to the airport tomorrow. Our cars will be delivered to Sonoma, and soon, we'll be sipping wine in warmer weather than this freezing hell in Chicago!"

I drew Rico close, sealing my words with a passionate kiss, communicating my boundless happiness. Rico couldn't resist injecting a note of practicality, "What about your family when they come for the wedding in June? Where are they going to all stay?"

I playfully hushed Rico with a finger to his lips, "Shh, I'm trying to seduce you into making love—just hush! I'm not called Smooth Tito for nothing!"

With that, we retreated to my bedroom, where we embraced in perfect harmony, ready to kickstart our new life… Or maybe just a gentle nudge.

The End